Arizona Heat

Cowboy Country, Volume 2

Lori Wilde and Pam Andrews Hanson

Published by L&P, 2021.

This is a work of fiction. Similarities to real people, places, or events are entirely coincidental.

ARIZONA HEAT

First edition. May 14, 2021.

ISBN: 979-8215356869

Written by Lori Wilde and Pam Andrews Hanson.

Table of Contents

Chapter One

SHE HAD TO BE HALLUCINATING.

Blame the hot desert sun in August.

For indeed, there couldn't be a naked man in a straw cowboy hat standing under the cascade of sparkling water. The fountain was in front of the Phoenix headquarters of the sporting goods company where Jane worked as administrative assistant to the CEO's executive assistant.

Jane Grant stopped and rubbed her eyes.

No way. That couldn't be a real guy. Too perfect. Had her boss' boss, the ostentatious Rupert Cox, added a statue of a nude cowboy to promote his new line of western-themed camping gear?

If that was the case, then she appreciated the spectacular eye candy. Grinning, she let out a low whistle.

She already loved the high-pressure jet of water, glowing like liquid gold as it caught the early-morning sun and fell into the surrounding pool. A cowboy was the perfect touch on this sweltering morning, his face raised as gleaming water splashed over a body so perfect that she let out a wistful sigh. Even from a distance, she saw the power in the statue's arms raised to clutch his thrown-back head and the chiseled grace of the golden torso.

If only real men looked like that!

She hurried toward the statue, eager to inspect the stunning piece of artwork before she rushed up to the penthouse offices where she worked. She did love art. At times like this, it wasn't so bad being a well-paid lackey. Even if the eccentric boss did begin his workday at the crack of dawn, often prompting her boss, Ms. Polk, to ask Jane to come in extra early, too.

Like today.

Suddenly, the statue moved.

Whoa!

Jane stumbled backward, pressing a hand against her heart. No, not a statue, after all. A random weirdo had indeed crawled into the fountain.

Alarmed, she glanced around. There wasn't a security guard in sight, and no other employees were here this early.

The interloper turned his back to the spray and brushed water from his face with the edges of his hands, doffed his straw cowboy hat, and slicked back a mane of wet hair. That's when she saw he wasn't naked and wore a pair of boxer briefs the same color as his golden flesh.

He was taking a shower in Rupert Cox's prized fountain. How dare he? Didn't he care if he got arrested for trespassing? She couldn't imagine being so cavalier, so bold, flaunting manners and convention.

"Oh, this is too much." She snorted. Jane followed the rules and expected others to do the same.

Too agitated to be afraid, she charged forward. Where did this guy get the nerve to use a beautiful ornamental fountain as his bathroom? If Mr. Cox saw him... She didn't even want to think of the CEO flipping his lid. What if he had another heart attack? She charged toward the trespasser, knowing she had to do something but not sure what.

"Hey, cowboy!"

He didn't answer. He probably couldn't hear her over the water.

"You can't do that here!" she shouted from the edge of the fountain.

She raised her voice, upping the volume to an attention-getting yell. "You can't take a shower here! Get out."

Slowly, he turned and spotted her, and his eyes lit up. He drilled her with his sultry stare.

Her heart flipped. She was unaccustomed to raw, primal men like him.

He settled the Stetson back on his head and came toward her, rippling bare muscles on full display, and she found herself wishing, ridiculously, that he'd turn around so she could see his backside. Water dripped down his flat, hard belly and his burnished bronze skin. A water droplet beaded on one chocolate-drop nipple as he raised his arms to squeeze more water from his hair.

Her womb contracted. What devilish sensation was this?

"This fountain belongs to the Cox Corporation. You can't bathe in it," she lectured, trying to sound as intimidating as Ms. Polk.

"I'm not bathing. See, no soap." The cowboy held out empty palms and gave her a head-to-toe ogle, not even trying to be subtle.

She squirmed, his steady gaze making her feel as exposed as he was. Worse, she felt like an idiot. It wasn't fair. He was a nearly naked trespasser, and she was doing him a favor by giving him a chance to vacate before she called the cops.

He started toward her, moving with unhurried insolence, his long, tanned feet visible now on the slippery aqua tiles lining the bottom of the pool.

"Look, if you're homeless, if you need a place to stay, I have a little money you can have, and a friend of mine volunteers at a mission—"

Good grief, Jane. There you go, tromping on boundaries; back off the caring nurturer instincts. He's not a lost puppy. He's not yours to save.

"Thanks, anyway. A bedroll is enough for me." He gestured toward a knapsack and rumpled sleeping bag on the other side of the pavement, flanked by a pair of workworn cowboy boots, jeans, and a western shirt.

"You don't understand. You can't camp out on Cox property."

"Oh?" He stopped a few feet away and looked her over again with deep-set blue eyes that shattered the last of her poise.

"You have to leave *now*."

"So, this Cox fellow... he's a hard-ass?" he asked.

"Yes—no... Not exactly..." Jane tried to back off the rim of the pool, not realizing how treacherous the wet marble could be until it was too late. She slipped, and her feet went out from under her.

"Oh!" she exclaimed, arms flailing.

Incredibly, he moved faster than she fell.

Instead of plunging forward and smashing her face in the shallow water as gravity and momentum intended, she was swept clear of the sharp edge and caught in powerful arms.

Instinctively, she clutched at shoulders as firm and smooth as well-worn saddle leather. Every nerve ending in her body came to life, shooting electricity through her limbs straight to her heart.

"Let go of me!" she cried.

"Steady now, darlin'," he drawled. "Get your footing. The bottom's slick as a newborn calf."

"I can manage." Jane tried backing away, but her left foot went out from under her, thrusting her leg awkwardly between the thighs that she was trying to avoid. His knees closed around hers, preventing another tumble but throwing her into a panic.

"Easy does it. You're fine. I'm not going to hurt you."

Maybe it was the drawl. The man's voice was oddly soothing in a sexy, deep-throated way. For whatever reason, she calmed down. He grabbed underneath her arms and lifted all five-foot-six inches of her over the rim of the pool.

She stood dumbfounded in the puddle dripping down her legs, shifting uneasily from one soggy shoe to the other.

"You can't sleep here either," she mumbled, picking back up where she'd left off before she'd fallen.

She did have a relentless quality that had landed Jane her much-coveted job. Looking over her shoulder at his makeshift bed, Jane gulped. Thinking about his sexy navel tucked in a nest of fine hairs that thickened at the waistband of the briefs.

Yikes!

Things like this didn't happen to Jane Grant, a twenty-six-year-old office worker and substitute mother to her younger sister, Kim. She'd taken over the role after their parents were killed in a plane crash nine years earlier. Her life was mundane with a capital *M* and would stay that way until Kim finished college in three years and got her teaching certificate.

Then and only then would Jane's life be her own.

"Seems I'm trespassing." The cowboy chuckled.

She didn't need to meet his gaze to know that he was grinning. She heard the humor in his voice. "I need to get to work, so could you please go?"

Jane glanced down at her neat, two-inch, bone-colored pumps and was pretty sure the discount footwear would dry into stiff, toe-pinching discards. Her calves were soaked, but at least her pastel-green dress had escaped all but a few splashes—and wet handprints where the cowboy had grabbed her.

"Sorry if I delayed you," he said. "I didn't expect anyone to be coming to work so early."

"Obviously not."

He sounded courteous enough, but she detected a twinge of amusement—maybe even irony—in everything he said. Was he making fun of her?

"I'm going into that building." Jane pointed at the large office complex with light-sand-colored walls and ornate cast-iron balconies not intended for use. "You have three minutes to disappear before I send security after you."

His grin broadened. He didn't look the least bit cowed.

Or contrite.

"Some of the guards are bigger than you. A lot bigger," she added.

"Thanks for the warning." The cowboy sauntered over to his gear and bent over to roll up the bed. Had he slept here?

She stared.

Good grief! The man was a masterpiece. His shoulders and back rippled with muscles under skin as smooth as polished copper. His waist was lean and his hips narrower than the breadth of his chest. She'd always poked fun at her friends when they rhapsodized over men's backsides, but this cowpoke's butt was world-class—full, round, muscular, and undulating as he

walked.

And his legs!

She could easily imagine them wrapped around her. Jane moistened her lips with the tip of her tongue.

Holy cattle drive!

She must be losing her mind. Policing the grounds wasn't in her job description, and Ms. Polk treated tardiness as one of the seven deadly sins. She had to go—now.

Ms. Polk was the walking caricature of a career woman from another era: short and scrawny, but big-busted with unfashionable tortoiseshell glasses, sweater sets, and salt-and-pepper hair pulled into a severe bun. She lived in dark skirts and probably owned several dozen white blouses, all of which were starched and ironed. The woman wore sensible stubby-heeled shoes and sometimes pinned a watch on her lapel to compare the time with that on her large wristwatch. She intimidated everyone but Rupert Cox. She would know how to handle a vagrant cowpoke.

Jane tried to ignore the squishing in her shoes as she hurried toward the building, not even indulging in another peek at the delicious hunk. With a bit of luck, she could slip off her pumps and let them dry while she hid out behind her desk.

"The clock starts now," she threatened and headed at a brisk pace toward her building. Behind her, she heard the man laughing.

Once she was inside, she told the security guard at the front desk about the cowboy and headed for the elevator.

When Jane reached the office three minutes late, Ms. Polk didn't even glance at her watch. She looked flushed and flustered. Jane had never seen Ms. Polk look either flushed or flustered. Wow, was the Cox Corporation on the brink of bankruptcy or something?

"Oh, yes, Jane, I forgot you were coming in early," the older woman said. "Busy yourself at your desk for a while."

Busy herself at her desk? No other instructions?

Huh?

For this, she'd gotten up at an unholy hour, steamed her eyes open in a hot shower, and drank three cups of black coffee to keep them that way. Something was radically wrong, but she knew better than to ply Ms. Polk with questions. She didn't want her head to be the first to fall into a basket under a downsizing guillotine.

Pausing, she went to the window to peek at the fountain, but no one was in sight: no security guard or the cowboy.

He'd gotten away in time.

Feeling irrationally disappointed that he'd disappeared, she plopped down at her desk and looked for busywork. If this was what it took to ingratiate herself to Ms. Polk, she would do it. The woman held the key to Jane's future. She couldn't get her dream promotion to the marketing department without Ms. Polk's approval.

Whatever the woman asked of her, she'd do it.

Jump through hoops? On it. Fetch coffee? You betcha. Sit behind a desk and pretend to work? I'm your woman.

Chapter Two

FINALLY, AT TEN O'CLOCK, her supervisor stopped in her doorway. "Jane, Mr. Cox wants to see you in his office."

"Mr. Cox asked for me?" The CEO rarely exchanged more than cursory greetings and had never asked for her personally.

Excitement coursed through her. Had Mr. Cox finally noticed her achievements? Could this be her toe in the door for getting that promotion and the much-needed income boost that went with it?

Ms. Polk didn't bother replying; she just slipped back through the crack in the door. A crack so small that Jane couldn't see into the opulent interior of the CEO's inner sanctum. The massive room was chocked with fat leather furniture, Persian rugs, and expensive Southwestern art.

Then another thought occurred to her. What if she was being called on the carpet? What if she'd done something wrong?

Forcing a smile, she hoped her face wouldn't freeze into an idiotic grin. After squaring her shoulders, she rapped lightly at the door before walking in. All she saw was the vast mahogany desk, the surface as smooth and shiny as glass, and the telescope Mr. Cox used to survey the grounds. Personally, she wondered why he simply didn't have a monitor installed into his office so he could watch the security cameras live.

"Join us over here, please, Jane," he boomed.

If Rupert Cox ever lost his financial empire, he could recoup his losses playing movie villains. He had a deep, compelling Darth Vader voice that gave her goosebumps whenever he directly addressed her, which was blessedly seldom.

Sprawled on a half-moon-shaped sofa, his feet propped on the surface of a polished ebony table, was the last man she ever expected to see again.

The naked cowboy.

Except now, he was fully dressed.

He caught Jane's eye and gave her a big wink as if they shared a secret. Panicked, she quickly glanced away. What was he doing in Mr. Cox's office, and how did his presence here affect her?

"We won't need you anymore, Ms. Polk," Cox told his executive assistant.

Ms. Polk gave a curt nod and marched toward the door, her spine and upper lip stiff. Jane wanted to beg the woman not to desert her, but Mr. Cox was already on his feet and ushering Jane into a nearby chair with a tight grip on her elbow.

She wasn't sure she cared for the high-handedness, but he was decent as far as bosses went. He might be eccentric, but she'd never gotten creepy vibes from him. So, although his pressure on her arm was just a little too firm, she didn't see it as harmful. He was just a forceful man.

Or maybe she was making excuses for his arrogance since she really wanted that promotion.

“Jane,” Mr. Cox said. "I’d like to formally introduce you to my grandson, Luke Black. He grew up in the wilds on a Montana cattle ranch and has since worked in Africa on a mission to end food insecurities in third-world countries.”

Was it her imagination, or did Luke wince at the introduction?

“I’m not as high-flautin’ or as untamed as grandfather likes to pretend I am.” Luke stood up, acknowledging Jane with a nod, and staring at her so intently she feared he might have developed X-ray vision.

He was even more dangerously disturbing with clothes on than without—not that what he was wearing could be called office attire. His Wrangler jeans were skintight and showed off his spectacular muscular thighs, and he’d apparently ripped the sleeves off a western shirt the same blue as his jeans. His feet didn’t look slender now in chunky cowboy boots. His hair had dried to a sandy brown with sun-bleached streaks of gold. And he seemed taller standing here in the office—at least six two.

"You’re from Montana, then?” she asked because some comment seemed to be expected from her. What was there to say to a handsome stranger after she’d seen him practically naked?

“I see you’ve dried off quite well.” Luke’s smile was wry. "Sorry to be the cause of your drenching.”

"Mmm, thank you.”

Silence. Well, that was awkward. What on earth was she thanking him for?

“Don’t get uncomfortable on my account.” Luke lowered himself back down on the sofa.

"Grandfather saw your valiant effort to eject a hinterlands cowboy from his fountain." He gestured at the high-powered telescope sitting on a tripod overlooking the front grounds.

"Damn cheeky, Luke," Mr. Cox said jovially. He seemed to be amused by his grandson's prank. "Playing in the fountain. Of course, you'll have to shape up after this. You can't keep acting like you're wallowing in some blasted glacier-fed watering hole."

His grandson didn't look intimidated, but Jane felt two inches tall with a feather for a backbone. She wanted out of here.

Why *was* she here?

She sat precariously on the edge of the antique chair. The upholstered leather seat was too slippery, and it rounded to accommodate her bottom. She crossed her legs at the ankle, all too aware of the still-damp shoes pinching her toes.

Luke examined her with hooded eyes, managing to look totally at home on a piece of

furniture that looked far too small for his big body, and he eyed her like she was a tasty buffalo, and he was Yellowstone gray wolf with hungry cubs to feed.

If she wasn't starved for that promotion, Jane would have leaped off the chair and run away as fast as her legs would carry her.

LUKE KNEW WHAT WAS coming and sympathized with the gorgeous blonde, even as he tried to cloak his amusement. Judging by her reaction to his early-morning dip in the fountain, he was expecting her to come unhinged when Gramps lowered the boom.

"Jane," Rupert began, sucking in his gut and throwing back his broad shoulders. "I'm not a young man, and after my heart attack two months ago, I've given some thought to retirement."

Jane.

Luke liked her name. Simple. Straightforward. Efficient. Competent. No nonsense. It suited her.

"Um, okay."

"Luke is my only living relative. His mom, my daughter, passed away when he was twelve, and because his father got custody, we haven't been in each other's lives as much as we would have liked."

Yeah, Luke thought. *That's one way of putting it.*

Another way would be that the old man hadn't really wanted anything to do with him. That is until Luke started gaining acclaim as one of the leading authorities on food insecurities in developing nations.

Rupert leaned back in his desk chair and rested his interlaced hands on his belly. "I want to be upfront with you, Jane. My daughter eloped to Montana with Peter Black, very much against my wishes. I had a suitable young man all picked out for her to marry, but she was headstrong and defied my wishes."

According to Luke's dad, Rupert had been a controlling son of a bitch that his mother, Meredith, had been desperate to escape. But that was one-sided. Luke was willing to give his grandfather a chance.

Their marriage lasted only a short time, and she ran off to find herself, only to die in a skiing accident in the Swiss Alps with a boy toy. She'd left Luke behind because he was too much of a handful."

Luke grimaced and shoved those memories aside. He was glad his mother had left him in Montana; she'd never taken much interest in him anyway.

But his father had never recovered from her desertion. Luke had loved growing up around rough-and-tumble cowboys while his father worked the ranch and hanging out with his cousins. Then Luke went off to college to get his undergraduate and master's degree in farm and ranch management. And he later spent eight years working for a nonprofit that served third-world countries struggling to feed their populations.

Peter Black began drinking too much and dabbling in conspiracy theories. His father hadn't believed the Covid-19 pandemic was real, and he refused to take precautions. In the end, his erroneous beliefs had killed him.

Not being there when his dad passed away was the most profound regret of Luke's life. He wasn't about to let that happen with his grandfather. When Rupert called, told him about the heart attack, and finally asked to see him, Luke jumped on a plane, leaving his life in the Congo behind.

Maybe if his father had lived, Luke wouldn't have been curious enough to answer his grandfather's summons. And for the record, it *had* been a summons and not an invitation, Luke realized now. Rupert was accustomed to being obeyed.

Luke was still feeling things out. He'd promised to stick around for a while and learn the business. Still, Luke had no interest in taking over the Cox Corporation. All he really wanted was to get to know his grandfather.

What he hadn't yet figured out was why Jane was here. What was the old man up to? Was he offering her up as a prize if Luke stayed?

C'mon, do you really think that little of him?

Hmm, maybe. Luke barely knew Rupert.

But Jane was a looker with hazel-green eyes, creamy skin, and honey-colored hair pulled back except for a few soft strands that had escaped and drifted around her heart-shaped face. Her entire lower lip had the smooth, plump look of a woman who should be kissed well and often. But she avoided his gaze, and he couldn't help feeling she was shy at heart. An introvert. He'd bet she loved books and reading—his total opposite.

"It's really lovely to meet you, Luke," she said, blinking all wide-eyed and innocent. She planted both hands on the arm of her chair and pushed up.

"Sit back down, Jane," Rupert commanded.

Like a well-trained pup, she sat.

"I have a favor to ask of you," Rupert said.

What did the old man have up his sleeve? Luke narrowed his eyes and glanced from his grandfather to Jane and back again.

"Yes, sir?"

"I want you to tutor my grandson."

"Excuse me," Jane and Luke said in unison.

Jane stared at Luke with questions in her eyes. He shrugged. He had no idea what was going on either.

Her forehead crinkled in a frown. "You want me to be Luke's what?"

"Tutor," Rupert confirmed. "And for the record, not only will you receive a generous bonus, but you are also the top candidate in the running for the opening we've got coming up in marketing."

Jane's eyes lit up, and Luke could see Rupert had found her kryptonite. *Money and position.*

Luke lost a little respect for her at that moment.

"I don't understand." Jane rubbed her upper arm as if she'd just gotten a painful injection. "What could I possibly teach your grandson?"

"It's straightforward, Jane. Before I hand over the company's reins to Luke, he needs to learn some basic etiquette and navigate the corporate environment. In short, I want you to civilize my grandson. He's spent too much time on ranches and in impoverished cultures to take over the reins of Cox Corp just yet." He sent Luke a chiding glance. "No more stunts like parading around naked in the fountain."

"Not quite naked," Luke said mildly, desperate to cloak his alarm. He had no intention of taking over as CEO. "I had underwear on."

"But why me? I'm not an etiquette expert." Jane sounded desperate to escape, and he couldn't blame her.

"You handled the situation in the fountain beautifully, Jane. You sent this rascal scampering for his clothes." He got up and walked over to pat his telescope. "I saw it all. He needs a handler."

Luke bit the inside of his cheek. People had been telling him that his entire life, and it didn't sting any less the millionth time than it had the first. People didn't say things like that to him in Africa, which was why he loved his adopted country.

Demurely, Jane ducked her head. "You give me far too much credit, Mr. Cox, I'm really not qualified to—"

"According to Ms. Polk, you're competent. Complete this assignment, and that position in marketing is yours, complete with a company car."

Jane's face paled.

It was all Luke could do to stay silent. He didn't want to pick a fight with his grandfather in front of Jane.

"Do we understand each other, Jane?" Rupert leveled her a knowing stare.

Jane fidgeted. Her eyes flashed, and her jaw set.

For a minute, Luke thought she'd tell his grandfather where he could stick the ridiculous assignment. He wished he had some popcorn to watch the fireworks, and he waited...

"Yes, sir."

Well hell. So much for fun.

"Splendid, splendid." Rupert sucked in his gut and slicked back his full mane of silver hair, reminding Luke of an aging wolf still fighting to lead the pack. The man was too accustomed to riding roughshod over people and getting his own way.

Really, Luke should walk out and grab the next plane back to Africa. The only thing stopping him was his stupid desire to find a way to connect with his grandfather before it was too late. After losing his father the way he had, Luke didn't want any more regrets.

"Do you have anything specific in mind for this transformation?" Jane took out her cell phone and opened a notetaking app.

Rupert tapped his chin with an index finger and glanced at Jane over the rim of his glasses. "Have you ever heard of the stage play *Pygmalion*?"

"Yes, sir. The movie *My Fair Lady* is based on it."

"Aah," he said. "You've chosen a timelier reference."

"Actually, sir, *My Fair Lady* is an older reference. *She's All That* is more to date, but even that movie was made in 1999."

She must be a killer at trivia night, Luke thought and didn't even bother stifling his grin. Yep, she had to be a reader. Something Luke was not.

"Whatever." Rupert waved a hand. "You get the idea. Give him a makeover—polish his rough edges. Teach him how to use a fork and knife. Show him how things work in the real world."

"Um, I'll see what I can do."

"You have thirty days. It'll be intensive. I'll have Ms. Polk arrange for you to use my ranch house in Sedona. You'll have an unlimited expense account to spruce him up—buy him some decent clothes. Get him a haircut and manicure too."

Jane's eyes grew wider still. "You expect me to—"

"Stay in Sedona with him. No distractions there. This is no forty-hour-a-week assignment, but you'll be extremely well rewarded for your troubles. Your bonus will be based on how well he turns out."

"Sir, it's not just about the money."

"Yes?" Rupert threw her a thundercloud frown.

"It's, it's—" The way she was floundering, Luke could tell it was precisely about the money.

"Just answer my question. Are you in or you out, Jane?"

She moistened her lip with a pink tongue. She looked from Rupert to Luke and back again and gulped visibly. "I'm in."

"Terrific," Rupert said. "I knew you were a team player. Go see Ms. Polk. She's making the arrangements for your departure."

"You mean right this minute?" Jane asked.

Rupert nodded. "Yes. Now get out of my office, both of you."

Chapter Three

"TELL ME MORE ABOUT the bronzed cowboy," Jane's younger sister Kim said as she watched her packing for Sedona.

"He's..." Pondering optional word choices, a few of them unkind, Jane finally settled on, "challenging."

"He sounds utterly fascinating. A wild Montana cowboy turned white knight for countries with food instability. I'm sold." Kim held a folded red tank top in her hands and added it to the pile of clothing waiting to go into the suitcase.

"Please take your tank out of my things. You know I never wear red," Jane said, eager to stop talking about Luke Black.

"I don't know why. The color makes you come alive."

"The last time I checked, I was definitely breathing." She usually wasn't sarcastic, but Kim was treating the whole thing as a lark. Her sister wasn't the one desperate for a promotion that could pay for a better neighborhood to live in.

"Wait. Is the guy a creeper? Are you afraid of him?" Kim didn't pull any punches.

"Oh, no, no. Not at all. Luke's just so...so—" Jane paused, casting around for the right word again.

"Masculine? Macho? Alpha?" Kim put the red top into the suitcase along with a yellow string bikini.

Jane was too agitated to protest the wardrobe additions. "No. Well, yes, he is those things and more."

Kim wriggled her eyebrows. "So, what's the problem?"

"He's smug. That's it—smug. You should see his smirk. He thinks he has the world on a string, and I suppose he does. He's poised to inherit a billion-dollar company, and he doesn't even seem to care."

"Mmm, I'd love to see him smirk. I'll go with you and help train him not to take showers in fountains." Kim giggled.

"There's an idea," Jane muttered, but she'd been a substitute mother too long to let her kid sister walk into trouble with her. "Unfortunately, you have classes starting soon."

"Rats. My loss. How long do you expect to be gone?"

"The entire month of August."

"Seriously? You'll be staying alone with a sexy cowboy for a whole month?"

"Oh no, we won't be alone. A couple lives on the ranch as caretakers, and company execs are scheduled to come down in two- and three-day shifts to teach him about the business. I'll just be his..."

"Governess?"

Jane laughed for the first time since Rupert Cox dropped the bombshell on her. "That's as good a title as any. To get my promotion, I must ride herd on a grown man who doesn't know what is and isn't appropriate in corporate America. Apparently, his mom—Mr. Cox's daughter—died when Luke was young, and he was raised on a Montana cattle ranch, and his dad let him run wild. Then he's spent his life since then in Africa. He doesn't know how to behave in the corporate environment. It's my job to tame his unruly ways."

"Wish I'd seen him in the fountain." Kim sighed moonily.

"Well, I wish *I* hadn't. Then I wouldn't be in this mess."

"Maybe he's a quick learner, and you can polish him up in less time," Kim mused. "Although I don't think I'd want to. What's so terrible about staying in Mr. Cox's fancy ranch hideaway in Sedona?"

"Being strongarmed into it," Jane muttered.

"Couldn't you have just said no?"

"I want that promotion."

"Yes," Kim said. "So, you can spend even more time working."

"What's wrong with that?"

"There's more to life than work, big sister. Open your eyes."

Easy for Kim to say. She wasn't the one who'd had to support them from the time she was seventeen years old.

"Look at it this way," Kim plopped onto the mattress beside Jane's suitcase. "You get a paid vacation."

"Vacation? With that guy? Ha. You have no idea how rough around the edges he is."

"Making a hot guy look good." Kim put the back of her hand to her forehead, feigning drama. "However, will you cope?"

Kim's curly-haired, dimpled cuteness was a magnet to the opposite sex. She often urged Jane to be more assertive and go after men who attracted her, but that wasn't Jane's style.

"I can understand why you're a charter member of the born-again virgins," Kim teased. "After your bad breakup with Bryan, I get it. But sister, it's time to get on with your life. That guy was a narcissist. You're far better off without him."

Jane knew that. She was just scared to take chances now. What if she got hooked up with the wrong man again? She picked up Mr. Hopper, the shabby stuffed kangaroo from her childhood, off the dresser and threw him at her sister.

Laughing, Kim ducked, and Mr. Hopper hit the wall with a soft *thud*. "C'mon, it can't be that bad. No one can blame you if the guy is totally not executive material. What have you got to lose?"

"A promotion," Jane said dryly. "Or if I totally blow it, even my job."

"Let me get this straight. You're off to spend a month tutoring a virile cowboy who oozes sex from every pore. He has a body worth giving up chocolate for and a dreamy face, but you don't want to go because he's too self-confident."

"Smug and cocky."

"Because he plays by his own rules, not anyone else's? Are you sure you're not just scared silly of having a close encounter of the romantic kind?"

"Don't you ever think about anything but men?"

Jane knew her question was unfair. Kim worked hard and got excellent grades. But she wasn't in the mood to be analyzed by her cheeky little sister.

Nor was she reassured by Kim's devious smile. If she didn't know better, she'd think her sister was up to something.

RUPERT'S SLEEK RED Ferrari had one helluva engine.

Grinning, Luke negotiated the switchback roads to Sedona with the skilled touch of a racecar driver. In fact, he'd driven in—and won—a few races and had briefly toyed with the idea of turning pro. But he'd gotten hooked on farm and ranch management. Ending world food insecurities and making a difference in people's lives was more rewarding than blasting around a track at top speed. But now, he was headed to his grandfather's Sedona ranch where he'd be sequestered with a gorgeous blonde as she attempted to teach him how to fit into "polite" society.

It was laughable.

He'd jump through the hoops—for now—because he had hopes of building a relationship with his only living grandparent. In the aftermath of Rupert's heart attack, he had no idea how long the old coot would be around.

Honestly, he had no intention of ever being CEO of Cox Corp. But if spending a month getting "tamed" by sweet Jane helped him forge a relationship with Rupert, he'd give it a shot.

Hanging out with Jane wouldn't be a sacrifice.

"Sly old devil," he muttered under his breath. "You caught me in your honey trap."

Was she in on his grandfather's plan to get him to stay in Arizona, or had Rupert decided to use her on the spur of the moment after the fountain incident? Him and his bloody spyglass!

Ahem. If you hadn't been in the fountain in the first place, none of this would have happened.

Okay, it had been a silly stunt meant to irritate Gramps. And yes, he still had some residual anger toward the man who'd never made much of an attempt to get to know Luke until he was ailing.

Thinking about Jane brought a smile to his face, and he decided she was probably just what she seemed. An employee roped into teaching him corporate-style manners. She hadn't been acting when she ordered him out of the fountain.

He was still disappointed that she'd insisted on driving her own car instead of riding to Sedona with him, but he got it. She didn't want to be stranded, and he couldn't blame her for that.

This promised to be an exciting month.

He'd expected plush digs, but the red rocks of Sedona were so spectacular under the hot August sun, he fantasized camping on a mesa with his bedroll. The landscape was a deep orange-red the color of burning coals, but the town itself was plagued with tourists who didn't have enough sense to take a siesta on such a hot afternoon.

Just off Highway 89-A, he approached his grandfather's ranch. The house had adobe walls and a heavy Spanish tiled roof, but it also had a security gate with a uniformed guard on duty. No riffraff was getting into the inner sanctum.

Well, except for him.

"Is Ms. Grant here yet?" Luke asked, stopping even though the guard had motioned him ahead as soon as he recognized the car.

"Yes, sir. She got here a couple of hours ago—"

"Much obliged," Luke said and roared on through. Dang, he did like the sound of the Ferrari's engine.

Leaving the sports car in the circular driveway, he quietly eased the door shut, stripped off his shirt, jeans, socks, and cowboy boots, and then locked his clothes in the trunk with his wallet and watch. Wearing nothing but a swimming suit—he was so ready for that infinity pool Rupert had told him about—he strolled to the house in flip-flops.

He'd asked Ms. Polk enough questions about the place to get the lay of the land. Nice woman, Polk, he thought, idly wondering whether her loyalty to his granddad went beyond the office. Rupert must have some hold on her, the way she scampered around, knocking herself out for the old man's every whim.

Jane too, for that matter. Because she'd been ordered to undo his bad habits. Habits honed from years raised on a Montana ranch, where he'd run free with his cousins and generally raised hell. His father had been too busy to pay attention, which had been most of the time.

"Good luck, honey." Luke grinned, thoroughly enjoying himself.

He ambled to the rear of the sprawling adobe house. It pleased him to see that Rupert had landscaped the place with rocks and cacti instead of trying to transform the desert into a phony version of Versailles. Which, quite honestly, he expected from the old man.

Luke found Jane lounging by the pool. Even at four o'clock, the sun was blistering hot, and she had sense enough to stretch out on a lounger shaded by a big red umbrella. He stopped, still concealed by the corner of the house, and studied her.

She *was* stunning.

Better still, she was alone and stretched out in a bright-yellow bikini, one knee drawn up and serving as a prop for her e-reader.

He'd recognize her legs anywhere: long, smooth, shapely. He speculated how it would feel to rub sunscreen from her cute little toes to the sleek fullness of her thighs, parted now with only a little bit of cloth between them. His imagination sparked like a torch set to dry kindling.

His luck couldn't be better.

Jane looked heavy-lidded and languid, only moments from falling asleep. What he really wanted to do was wait until the e-reader fell, a sign she'd fallen asleep, and wake her with a kiss.

Horrible idea! Too personal. A clear boundary violation.

He didn't want her scurrying back to Phoenix. The next tutor his grandfather sent might not be so much to his liking. But he wanted her to look at him and not her book.

Grinning, he yelled, "Cannonball," kicked off his flip-flops, ran toward the pool, and plunged.

Jane shrieked.

He swam, slicing through the tepid water with powerful strokes, performing for her and immensely enjoying every lap. He was at his best when he was in motion. After ten fast laps, he looked over to the concrete apron of the pool.

"You're not funny," she said, bending forward so her words carried to him loud and clear. "You startled me, and it's an attention-getting trick a ten-year-old would pull. If you think I'm going to run back to Phoenix because of your childish stunts, you're in for a surprise, Mr. Black."

Treading water near her feet, he looked up and grinned guilelessly. "Sorry I acted like a crazed bull bustin' out of the pasture," he said. "I just had to go for it."

"Do wild bulls splash in swimming pools?" She was sharp, this one, and he liked her even more.

"Join me," he invited.

"No, thanks."

"Ahh, c'mon. Our whole relationship is water-based."

"We don't have a relationship. I'm your instructor."

"And none too pleased about it."

"I like my job, and I need to keep it."

"Point taken." Luke watched, timing his move for the exact moment she turned to walk away.

If she hadn't been so mad at him for scaring her, she might have seen it coming. He pulled her into the pool, sending her plunging back into the water with him.

She came up sputtering, angry enough to spit nails. "You have no right to do that."

"I apologize, Janie," he said, realizing too late he'd made a big mistake. As much as he liked her, she was right. They weren't teenagers, and he'd acted like an idiot. His impulsiveness strikes again.

"I'm Ms. Grant to you."

He hung his head, pretending more shame than he felt. "I'm a doofus."

"Yes, you are."

"What can I say? I was raised on a ranch around a bunch of men. I have no manners. It's kind of why I'm here."

Sporting a suddenly wicked grin, she splashed hard, sending a wave of water breaking over his head.

"Don't start what you can't finish, Ms. Grant," he warned, thrilled that she wasn't quite as mad as she looked.

He dove, and she started to climb from the pool, managing to get her arms and one knee over the edge before he struck.

She anticipated his maneuver and ducked.

Instead of pulling her back down, he lightly tickled the back of her knees.

She squirmed and squealed.

Ahh, she was ticklish.

"Hands off, cowboy," she growled, scrambling the rest of the way up the ladder, then turning to glare down at him.

He raised his palms in surrender.

"Don't ever touch me without my permission again." Jane chuffed out her breath. "Consider that your first lesson in being civilized. Women don't like to be manhandled."

This time he was genuinely chagrinned. "I can see where my friskiness might be unwanted. I didn't mean to stomp on your boundaries."

"Thank you," she said. "But don't let it happen again." She tossed her wet hair over her shoulders, stalked to the house, and disappeared through the sliding glass doors.

What the devil was he going to do here with her for an entire month? The familiar feeling of being trapped settled over him. It was the same feeling that had made school so difficult for him. He wasn't the kind of person who could sit still for long.

He was, as his mother had often stated in the years before she walked out the door, a handful.

Now here he was, stuck for a month with a sexy woman who could give a disapproving schoolmarm a run for her money, with nothing to do but learn how to mind his manners.

Ugh.

It was going to be a long, hot August.

Chapter Four

WHERE WAS HER NAVY-blue dress?

Jane searched her suitcase as she unpacked, but the dress wasn't there. Had her sneaky little sister slipped it out of the garment bag when she wasn't looking?

"Kim, what did you do?" she muttered.

Jane loved that dress, even if her sister did call it "the date dampener." Now, when she really needed something high-necked, loose-fitting, and ankle-length, she was left staring at Kim's white halter dress.

"That little sneak," Jane muttered, but it wasn't her sister's wardrobe games that had her two seconds away from bolting.

How on earth could she have any influence on a man so rambunctious and uninhibited and sexy and—

Her cheeks got hot just thinking of lying on her belly on the hard wet concrete while a man she barely knew had tickled the backs of her knees.

He was *wild*, that long, tall cowboy.

And for the next month, he was her problem unless she wanted to kiss that promotion goodbye—not exactly an appealing option.

How was she going to get through this?

"By not playing Luke Black's game," she muttered, hanging up a pair of beige linen slacks.

At least Kim hadn't taken her bulky white cotton cardigan she'd brought for cool desert nights. Buttoned to the neck over a tank top, it would send a message as well as the navy dress—*keep your distance, buster.*

But here was the thing she didn't want to admit, not even to herself. When Luke had teasingly pulled her into the pool, she'd liked it.

And she'd liked it even more when he'd stroked the back of her knees with his calloused fingertips. That's why she'd overreacted. It wasn't what he'd done so much as the way he'd made her feel.

Oh, who was she kidding? She liked *him.*

And that was a huge problem.

Luke wasn't the one who needed a keeper. It was she.

Feeling entirely unlike herself, she stepped to the window, and she opened the blinds to let some sunshine in, hoping to chase away the weird sensations bombarding her. She liked Luke Black, but she didn't want to like him.

Simple as that.

She cast a glance out the window as she walked away, caught movement from her peripheral vision, did a double take, stopped, and walked backward to stare.

My dear heavens, what was the lunatic doing now?

Answer to that question? He was handwashing Rupert's Ferrari in soaking wet swim trunks. His bare torso was covered with soapy bubbles, and he rubbed the car back and forth in languid circular motions.

She ogled utterly and unabashedly, and her imagination caught fire.

Just tell the truth, Jane.

Okay, fine, her fantasies exploded. In her head, she heard cheesy porno music, and her toes curled. Luke bent over the hood of the red-hot sports car, giving it a thorough scrubbing.

Jane sucked in her breath, overwhelmed by pure, sweet lust. In her mind, she was that sleek hunk of metal, and Luke's hands were on her—caressing, stroking, massaging.

She raked her gaze down his body. Beginning at the top of his shaggy golden-brown hair, just long enough to be pulled back with a tie and slid on down over the sharp angles and honed bones of his exquisitely muscular frame. This was not a man who spent any time tucked inside an office.

He was as free as a wild animal, and Rupert Cox wanted her to wrangle him into the zoo of corporate America.

A deep sadness settled into her stomach. Was the promotion worth it?

It's a twenty-thousand-dollar-a-year raise and a company car.

Right. Whatever was going on between Luke and his grandfather was not her problem. She had a job to do, and she would do it.

Luke Black could darn well sort out his family issues on his own.

SAUNTERING THROUGH the downstairs rooms, Luke found himself admiring the house more than he cared to admit. He liked the rough plastered walls tinted the color of desert sand, the gleaming hardwood floors, and Navajo rugs in black, red, yellow, and turquoise. There were giant earthenware pots with broad-leaved plants, black leather couches, and chairs comfortably indented from extended use. There were heavy carved wooden tables with lamps and odd bits that looked like prized possessions, not some decorator's arty idea of accessories.

The caretaker's wife, Wilma, kept everything polished like a new sports car, but the place still had a homey, lived-in vibe.

He slumped into an overstuffed chair and let one leg hang over a plush arm, wondering how much longer it would be before Jane came down the iron spiral staircase. Had he overdone the untamed cowboy schtick? He was undoubtedly rattled. Who knew a tickle on the back of her knees would have the impact of dynamite?

On them both.

He waited, wondering what he'd do if she didn't show. His first impulse was to carry a dinner tray to her room and apologize again for overstepping her boundaries. But wouldn't that be going too far as well?

What he knew about sophisticated women like Jane wouldn't fit in the palm of his hand. The soft click of heels on the staircase carried down to him. He fixed his gaze on the steps as Jane slowly descended, hanging on to the railing.

Mouth going dry, he followed her progress, taking in the graceful steps and the way her dark-sable hair framed her face. As for her sensational legs, he could only remember them as he'd seen them at the pool because they were nowhere in sight. She'd wrapped herself up like a mummy, swathed in baggy slacks and a bulky sweater.

Aww, damn.

He stood up, wondering how close she'd get to him. "Won't you get too warm in that sweater?"

"Not at all." Her airy tone didn't fool him; she was hiding her body from him, and he supposed he was to blame for that.

He shouldn't have tickled her knees. He'd acted like a troglodyte, and now her legs were off-limits.

"It'll get chilly after the sun goes down," she added.

"Which doesn't happen for a couple more hours."

"Is that your idea of proper dinner attire?" Her tone brought the temperature down a few degrees as her gaze raked over him.

"This is the only suit I brought. Sorry about the wrinkles." He pretended to examine the many creases in his white linen jacket.

"I meant the Wranglers. Do you *always* wear jeans?"

"I could take them off." He hitched and moved a hand to his zipper as if he intended on shucking off his clothes right here, right now.

Her cheeks pinked, and she sighed. "I know you're teasing me, but jeans are inappropriate for a business dinner."

"Maybe around here, but in Montana—"

"But we're not in Montana, are we?"

"I thought Arizona was cowboy country too."

"It's fine tonight because we're alone, but in the future, especially when others are dining with us, please wear a real suit."

"C'mon, you're telling me no one wears jeans in a corporate office?"

"No."

"Gramps owns a sporting goods store. Why can't I look like a customer?"

"No."

"Why not?"

"You're special. You're a Cox."

"I'm a Black," he growled.

A tiny frown creased her forehead, but she kept her voice cool, calm, and collected. "Look, your grandfather hired me to teach you how to act and dress like a CEO. You've already got the cowboy thing down pat. Let's stick to the plan and bolster your weaknesses."

"I'm wearing a tie." He tried for a beguiling grin, fiddling with his bolo tie. "Do I get points for that?"

Her frown deepened. "A bolo doesn't classify as a proper corporate tie."

"Want to know a secret?"

"I'm terrified to say yes," she said, her tone as dry as the arid desert around them.

"Psst," he whispered. "I don't know how to tie a real tie."

"Why am I not surprised? I'll go check Rupert's closet and see what I can find. When I return, I'm going to teach you how to properly tie a tie. That'll be your first lesson."

"Fine by me."

Cocking his head, Luke watched her sashay back up the stairs. The view was just as appealing going as coming. Luke draped himself over the chair again, gleefully awaiting her return. He could observe her all day long and never get bored.

And for a guy who got restless quickly, that was saying something.

"WHAT AM I LETTING HIM do to me?" Jane muttered aloud as she stared at the rack laden with expensive silk ties mounted on the back of the closet door in Rupert's bedroom.

Railing against his bolo tie, she'd sounded like a prim spinster who believed her way was the only way. Why should she care if he looked like a cartoon cowboy? All she had to do was ignore him as much as possible for a month—twenty-nine days to be exact since it was August second. How long was that in hours? Minutes?

"Pick a tie, any tie," she muttered.

Easy to say, but what tie went with a white linen jacket, black-and-white-striped western shirt, and starched denim?

Um, nothing.

If Rupert's clothes fit Luke, she'd send him up here to change, but his grandfather was three sizes larger than Luke.

Finally, she decided on a simple black tie. No pattern. No other color. It was boring. Not a thing like Luke would ever wear.

It was perfect.

She went back downstairs to find him staring into the salt-water aquarium built into the stone wall of the fireplace. He turned to her as she entered the room, tie in hand.

Crossing toward him, she tried to ignore how her pulse quickened the closer she got. Silliness.

There you go again, acting like an old maid.

She was young and single, and so was he. He was sexy and handsome. Nothing wrong with facing facts. If it was any other guy, she'd let her fantasies run amok. To be honest, they already were.

His butt did look great in those jeans.

Ahem.

He was the boss' grandson who might soon be taking over the company. Did she really want to go there?

No, no, she did not.

I do, whispered a long-dormant part of her she'd set aside while she'd been raising Kim. She'd lost out on a lot of hookups because of her baby sister.

Luke strolled closer, easing off his bolo tie as he sauntered with those tanned, calloused fingers. With each swivel of his smooth hips, her heart pounded faster. By the time he reached her personal space, she'd thought she might levitate from the sheer force of the pounding.

His smile was cocksure.

He extended his neck. "Tie me up."

"Wh-what?" She could scarcely get the word out.

"Lay it on me."

"Wh-what," she stammered again, her mind vapor locked.

"Show me how it's done."

> Dear God, she was so out of it. His scent, his smile, his gorgeous eyes mesmerized her. Too close. He was entirely too close.

But instead of backing up and regrouping, she stupidly went up on her tiptoes so she could loop the black silk tie around his neck. She prattled, "There are seventeen different ways to tie a tie."

"You're kidding me."

"Not at all. There's the Windsor, the half-Windsor, the four-in-hand, the pra—"

"You sure know a lot about ties." His breath smelled so good. Minty. He had to have just brushed his teeth or sucked on a peppermint. "What did you do? Work in a menswear store or something?"

"Something like that," she murmured.

He didn't need to know her life history. Or that she'd once dated the CFO of a major corporation, and that's how she knew what a terrible idea it was to date your boss.

"Did you know..." She kept jabbering to keep her mind off his intoxicating cologne. "You should choose to knot your tie based on the image you wish to project?"

"I did not know that. Gimme a for instance."

"Stronger leaders usually tie a full Windsor. Men like your grandfather. A full Windsor is presidential."

"Hmm."

She went on. "There's tie knots for tall guys, short guys, big guys, skinny guys..."

"Get outta here. Really?"

"Truth. Some knots work better for certain body types. Generally, most men prefer the four-in-hand."

"I'm not most men, Jane," he said in a low voice so hot and sultry a shiver knifed through her.

Was that a warning or an invitation?

No warning necessary. Jane was already as wary of him as an escaped zoo tiger. Only in this case, Rupert Cox had made her a very unwilling animal trainer.

"Still, this is the customary knot," she said, ignoring her trembling knees. "Please pay attention. You loop this end around here..."

He wasn't paying attention. His gaze was fixed right on Jane's mouth.

"Oh, you know what?" she said, flustered. "You're right. Stick with the bolo. It suits you."

"No, no," he said. "You've caught my interest. Teach me the ways of the tie, sensei. I'd be interested in seeing all seventeen versions. Maybe you could show me one knot every night for the next seventeen nights..."

"Master the four-in-hand first," she said, putting steel into her voice. "Watch me."

"I'm watching."

"Not my face, my hands."

"Oh, was I staring?"

"You know you are."

"Hey." He shrugged. "Not my fault you're gorgeous."

"Okay, that's it. I'm out." She stuck the tie in his jacket pocket and turned away.

He grabbed her wrist.

She glared. "What did I tell you about touching me uninvited?"

He dropped her hand immediately and offered a contrite grin. "Rupert warned you. I need civilizing. I apologize for being an oaf. Please show me the four-in-hand thingy."

"Dinner is ready," Mrs. Homing announced from the doorway on the far side of the room. "Service on the patio grotto."

"The knotting lessons will have to wait," Jane said, relieved.

"You're a sweetheart, Wilma," Luke called to Mrs. Homing. "I'm so hungry, I could eat a horse."

Wilma Homing beamed at Luke's flattery, and Jane crossed the caretaker's wife off her concise list of potential allies. Would her husband, Willard, be taken in by Luke's rakish charm, too?

Jane had the uncomfortable feeling Luke was playing some kind of game, and she didn't know any of the rules.

Chapter Five

JANE LED THE WAY THROUGH the recreational room, past the ornate antique billiard table, pinball machines, and shuffleboard, and opened the sliding glass door to the pool area.

"Hold up, Janie."

She wished he wouldn't call her that. It sounded way too familiar. He held out his elbow for her to take his arm.

"Shouldn't I escort you instead of you racing ahead of me? Isn't that proper etiquette?"

He had a point. Jane hesitated, but it seemed rude to leave him hanging. Begrudgingly, she slipped her arm through his.

"Thanks," he whispered.

"What for?"

"Accepting my chivalrous gesture."

She snorted. "Is that what you're calling it?"

Laughing, he guided her along a path of terracotta tiles. Even though her bulky knit sweater made it as impersonal as a handshake, she stiffened underneath his touch. The sun was still a fiery orb in the sky, affording no letup in the relentless summer heat.

Sweat pooled in her cleavage. Who knew cotton could be so warm?

They rounded the corner to the west end of the big stucco house. Arbor grapevines created a nifty little cave on the back side of the pool waterfall. They could see an unobstructed view of the famous Sedona red rocks through the open end of the grotto. It looked more like a movie set than real life.

The grotto itself had just enough space for a small redwood table shaded by the thick grapevines. Sitting knee to knee, four people could share the table, but Jane felt crowded when Luke seated her at a heavy wooden deck chair with bright flowered cushions and took his place across from her.

His knee brushed hers as he slid the chair closer to the table, and he mumbled, "Sorry," which did nothing to relax her.

Their places were set with an intimidating number of gleaming silver forks and heavy geometric-patterned china dishes in shades of turquoise and orange. The table was covered by a pale-peach linen cloth, with the matching napkins monogrammed *R.C.* A slender-lipped bottle sat in a silver bucket filled with ice.

"Wine with a cork," Luke mused, picking up a corkscrew opener and examining the mechanism. "My guess is, I'm supposed to decant and pour."

If he knew enough to do that, why did he need etiquette lessons from her? Now, if he'd cracked the bottle across the table, broken the neck off, and taken a swig, she could offer some helpful advice—like try not to cut yourself on the jagged edges.

Instead, she said nothing and concentrated on sliding the elegant linen napkin across her lap.

Luke stood up to tackle the cork. The top snaps on his western shirt were undone, given her a glimpse of his bronze chest. When had the snaps come undone? His shirt had been closed when she'd been trying to put on his tie. Was the gap intentional, or did the snaps simply close poorly?

She didn't know where to focus her eyes. Fortunately, Willard Homing came pushing through the door at the end they'd come out of, carrying a silver tray.

"Fresh prawns," he announced.

"Fancy," Luke drawled the last syllable, admiring the giant pink prawns served in a crystal dish set inside a larger plate of crushed ice.

"It has to be for our Mr. Cox," Willard said, resting his hands on the front of the white apron covering his rotund Buddha belly. "And you in turn by association."

"Good job, Will. Top-notch service."

"Very nice, yes, thank you, Mr. Homing," Jane agreed, a little miffed because Luke was much more at ease with the staff than she was. What on earth was she supposed to teach him?

She felt more and more like a ploy to keep Rupert's grandson entertained than any real mentor.

Worse, she was hot enough to spontaneously combust.

Her face had to be pinker than the prawns, and the sweater was sticking to her shoulder blades like a wet rug. She tried to push up her sleeves inconspicuously as Willard was leaving, but sharp-eyed Luke noticed.

"Are you sure you don't want to slip out of that sweater, Janie?"

"I'm fine."

"Suit yourself." He grabbed a giant prawn with his fingers, dunked it in spicy red sauce, and made it disappear, tail and all, in one big bite.

"Ahem." She looked at him pointedly and picked up the delicate silver cocktail fork at the outer end of the lineup of flatware on her left and tapped it lightly on the edge of the rice dish. "We start from the outside and move in with each course. This will be important at business luncheons."

"What? Using extra water on washing a bunch of silverware when one fork would do?" He frowned. "Corporate America is wasteful."

"That's not the point."

"It's precisely the point." He popped a second prawn into his mouth and chewed with gusto. At least he didn't eat with his mouth open. That was something.

"Try one," he invited, pushing the tail out of his mouth with the tip of his tongue and planting it beside the first tail in the mound of ice.

Gritting her teeth, she said, "Allow me to demonstrate how it's done."

"Have at it." He waved a hand and looped a lazy arm around the top of his chair.

She forked a prawn and brought it to the small appetizer plate that Willard had brought. Using a fork and knife, she cut off the tail and discreetly moved it to the left side of her plate.

Luke rolled his eyes. "Like that is so much better."

"You try it."

"Fine." He duplicated her actions, flawlessly executing the proper way to handle a prawn with the tail served on it.

"Good job."

"Do I get a gold star now?"

"Don't tell me you don't have forks in Montana or Africa," she said.

"Depends on whether I'm feasting on grubs from under a fallen log, or sopping up gravy with chuckwagon biscuits, or dining with a politico who needs softening up to grant me the right permits."

Surely, he was kidding about the grubs.

Stricken, she dropped the fork, wondering whether she might pass out from heat or squeamishness. Either way, she was about to faint.

"JANE?" WORRY YANKED at Luke.

She didn't look so good.

He shouldn't have said that about the grubs. He'd only been kidding.

Her skin paled, and she put a hand to her mouth as if trying not to throw up.

Dammit, Black, show some common sense.

"Jane?" he repeated. "Speak to me."

She didn't answer.

"Are you okay? I was just kidding. I don't really eat grubs. It's a joke. Haha. Yes, not funny."

She blinked and took a deep breath. "I'm fine."

"You don't seem fine."

Sweat broke out on her brow, and she pressed a palm to her forehead.

"Have a drink." He stood, picked up her water glass, and held it out to her.

She downed a few good swallows but didn't look much better. "I'm sorry, one shouldn't gulp their beverage. Do as I say, not as I do."

Seriously? She was still trying to teach him manners?

"Maybe you got overheated. You'd better peel the sweater off before you pass out. It's hotter than I expected when I told Wilma we'd eat in the grotto." He pantomimed, undoing an imaginary sweater, and throwing it over his shoulder.

Her eyes were glazed.

"Do you want me to help you out of the sweater?" Alarmed, he got up and moved toward her.

She swatted his hand away. "No, leave me be. I'm just a little dehydrated. All I need is more water."

He reached for the crystal water pitcher and refilled her glass. She gulped the whole thing and let out a soft burp.

"Oops, my goodness." She put three fingers over her mouth. "That was exceptionally rude of me."

"Not at all. Burping is good for you. Burp away, Janie."

She gave him the stink eye.

Okay, so she wasn't ready to joke. "You sure you don't want to take off your sweater?"

"Why are you trying to undress me?"

"I'm not. I just want you to cool off."

"I can take care of my own body heat. Thank you very much."

He sat down, leaving the chair some distance from the table so he could stretch his legs, lean back, and study her in comfort. Putting space between them was good. Scaring her off wasn't. Not only because he really liked her, but if Jane bolted, Rupert would most likely send Ms. Polk to take her place.

Straighten up and fly right, Black.

"How about this," he said, gifting her with what he hoped was a billion-dollar smile. "If I promise to behave myself, will you take off that Arctic survival wear, relax, and enjoy a nice dinner?"

"Depends on your idea of behaving." She narrowed her eyes.

God, she was suspicious. "I'll begin by apologizing for the bit at the pool again. I shouldn't have tickled the back of your knees. I violated your personal space, and it's made things tense between us."

"That's a start," she said but kept the sweater on.

"I'll call you Ms. Grant and use every fork in the lineup," he cajoled, seriously worried about her health. Why did she insist on wearing a sweater for crying out loud? She had a gorgeous body. Why was she hiding it? "I promise."

"Oh, finish your prawns." Sighing, she surreptitiously slipped her arms from the sweater and let it drop from her shoulders to bunch up behind her razor-straight back.

Do not stare at her chest.

He caught her gaze and held it, refusing to glance down when that's all he wanted to do. He would not be *that* guy.

"So, Jane," Luke said, using his fork and knife to dissect the prawn the way she'd showed him and dipping it into the remoulade sauce. "Tell me about yourself."

"Not much to tell." She pierced him with one of her stony stares. "My parents died when I was seventeen, and I applied for guardianship of my little sister. I went to work to support us, and I've been working hard ever since."

She babbled as if the speed at which she told the story would lessen her pain.

"I'm sorry for your loss. I'm an orphan too." He told her a bit about his history.

"Being orphaned young is a terrible thing for us to have in common." She shook her head.

"You're luckier. At least you have a sister," he murmured and then realized that made him sound like 'poor me,' which was not his intention.

"I know how lucky I am," she said. "Kim is the best."

She talked about her younger sister for a bit, and he could tell how much Jane loved her. He felt a pang that he hadn't had a sibling. Then again, he'd had his cousins Mitchell and Able, and that had been almost as good.

While they were talking, Willard brought out the second course, a tangy gazpacho. After Willard departed, Jane showed Luke how to dip his spoon into the soup and pull the spoon away from him to scoop it up.

"As you lift your spoon, make sure to gently touch the underside of the spoon against the far edge of the bowl," she instructed.

"Like this?" He demonstrated.

"Nicely done," she praised.

"I can see how this method would prevent getting soup on my shirt."

"How come your dad never remarried after your mom left?" she asked, easing back into the conversation.

"Not much opportunity for mates in the wilds of Montana," he said. "I was raised in River Falls, population one thousand twelve or thereabouts."

"Do you ever go back home?"

"Once in a while to visit my cousin, Mitchell. We were running buddies back in the day, along with our other cousin,

Able. Able is a Texas Ranger, and he lives in Austin." Luke paused.

"Mitchell is like you. Both his parents were killed in an automobile accident, and he had to raise his younger brothers."

"That's way too much tragedy in one family. Mitchell's parents. Your parents."

"Mitchell says the Blacks are not just survivors, but thrivers. I have to agree."

"I like Mitchell already."

"Don't like him too much." Luke chuckled. "He just got engaged to the love of his life. I'm so happy for him. Ann is a lovely woman."

"You sound like you have a lot of affection for your cousin." Jane's face softened.

"Yeah." Emotion pushed against his chest. His early life had been rough, but no harsher than Jane's, he supposed.

"What about Able? Is he orphaned too?"

"Nope. He's got a big nuclear family, and that's where Mitchell and I hung out. His mom is the best cook." Luke lowered his voice. "Even better than Mrs. Homing."

"That's a claim to fame. The housekeeper a great cook, and this gazpacho is the best I've ever had."

"Shifting the topic," Luke said, aching to know more about Jane. "What do you do for fun when you're not tutoring uncouth cowboys in the ways of the corporate world?"

Jane shrugged. "I don't have much time for myself. I often work fifty hours a week or more and looking after Kim—"

"Who's in college," he pointed out.

"You're right." She surrendered a slight smile. "I've been using Kim as an excuse to put my life on hold. I know I should get out more, date more, but honestly..." She shrugged. "I'm content."

"But not happy."

"I didn't say that."

"Are you?"

"What?"

"Happy."

"As much as the next person, I guess."

"In other words, no?" he teased.

"Are *you* happy?"

"You bet I am." He paused. "When I'm not being ordered around by a money bags grandfather I don't even know."

"Rupert means well. He only wants what's best for you."

"Does he?"

That brought Jane up short. "Of course."

"You sure about that?"

"He's your grandfather."

"Who really didn't want much to do with me until he had a heart attack. Suddenly, he wants to be big buddies as if the past thirty years of radio silence never happened?"

"I can tell this is a sore spot."

"You think?"

"Why are you here then?"

"Other than my cousins, he's my only living relative." Luke wished he hadn't brought up the topic. He didn't want to talk about his grandfather. "You look gorgeous in the sunset, Jane."

"You want me to shut up about your relationship with Rupert?"

He shrugged and gave her a sheepish grin. "Yes, but you really are stunning."

Her cheeks reddened, and she ducked her head, finishing the last bite of chilled soup. He hoped it had cooled off her heatwave.

Willard brought out the main course. Pan-seared duck, fingerling potatoes, and asparagus. It looked like a gourmet meal. The food was delicious, and beyond the etiquette lessons, they didn't speak. Jane told him to entirely focus on enjoying the meal, and so he did.

It wasn't until Willard brought the dessert of fresh raspberries in chocolate sauce and whipped cream that the conversation turned personal again.

Unfortunately, Jane asked a question he didn't really want to answer.

"So, tell me," she said. "Why isn't a handsome man like you already married?"

Chapter Six

AAH, THE QUESTION THAT never failed to crop up for the women he dated. Why wasn't he married?

Why?

Short answer? He'd never found a woman who could hold his interest beyond the chemical romance stage.

Longer answer? He'd never found a woman who could hold his interest beyond the chemical romance stage, plus he was swamped helping to stomp out starvation, plus he honestly didn't know how to sustain a long-term relationship, plus—

Truthful answer? He was making excuses because he was terrified of commitment. His mother had bolted when he was twelve, leaving him behind because his boisterous behavior was too much for her to handle. He couldn't help thinking that meant he was too much of a handful for any woman.

That's why he didn't want commitment—the dreaded fear of rejection. But no way in hell was he going to eviscerate himself and spill his guts in the Arizona desert to a woman he barely knew.

He latched his gaze on to Jane's and answered her question as succinctly as he could. "Not interested."

"In marriage?"

He shrugged.

"Why not?"

"Do I have to have a reason?"

"You do have one, whether you admit it or not, but you don't have to answer. I was just curious."

He considered that for a moment, then said, "I'm just not marriage material."

Jane snorted. "What does that even mean?"

Damn, but the woman was relentless. He focused on her pink tongue, flicking out to lick the last bit of chocolate from the tines of her fork, and felt his body tighten.

"Luke?"

"It means I don't want to talk about it." Shifting gears to dampen his arousal, Luke turned in his chair to admire the sunset and ignore the thumping of his pulse. "Can we drop it?"

"The rock formations are stunning," Jane said, thankfully letting go of the irritating topic.

"They are. I can't stop staring at the rocks. They're mesmerizing."

"Is this your first time in Sedona?"

"It is."

"No kidding?" She sounded surprised. "I figured since you're a cowboy, you would have visited your grandfather's ranch a lot."

"My grandfather and I aren't close."

"I'd gathered that, but I thought perhaps you'd visited the ranch anyway when you were a kid."

"Nope."

"You missed out on the red rocks."

"I did. I've seen the rocks in movies, of course, but it's a totally different experience seeing them up close and personal."

He felt the tension in his body ebb as they discussed the landscape.

"It is," Jane agreed and paused for a moment as if hatching a plan. "Maybe we could go on a Jeep tour of the area at some point."

He turned back to face her. "Really? That sounds amazing. Let's do it."

"All right, but business first. There are other things we need to take care of before a Jeep tour, like shopping."

"Shopping for what?" He hated shopping and his muscles tuned up again at the thought of it, tightening across his chest and abdomen.

"You need business suits for your meetings."

Luke groaned. "Are you kidding me? We're on a ranch. Why can't I dress like a cowboy?"

"As darling as your western image is," she said with genuine admiration in her voice. "You're representing Rex to his underlings, and that means you have an image to uphold. You are the heir apparent, not a ranch hand."

If his grandfather wasn't ailing, Luke would have just said no. This was beyond ridiculous, putting on a monkey suit in the desert, and for what? To try to impress other men in monkey suits in the desert.

"You really haven't had much experience in corporate America, have you?" She looked at him as if a UFO had just dropped him off and disappeared into the night. Sometimes, he felt as if he *was* an alien from another planet.

"Zero." He grunted. "From a Montana cattle ranch to resolving food insecurities in Africa, I've never even worked indoors. Psst, don't tell anyone, but I've never owned a suit. The few times I've needed one, like for wedding and funerals, I've rented them."

A knowing smile flitted across her face. "You're a rare bird, Luke Black."

"I'll take that as a compliment."

"I meant it as one." She canted her head and studied him with a pensive look on her face as if she was trying to figure out what made him tick.

That look put a tickle in his belly, and he didn't know why. "Would you like to go for a stroll on the grounds?"

"Sure." She smiled, and with that smile, he felt like she'd gifted him the world. "That sounds nice."

He glanced down at her feet. "Would you like to change your footwear? I could clear the table while you change."

"How far are we going? These pumps are surprisingly comfortable, and if we don't walk for long, I should be fine."

"Fifteen minutes?"

"That sounds perfect. I'll help you bus the dishes."

It was getting cooler now that the sun had gone down, and she put her sweater back on. After they carried their dishes into the kitchen where Mrs. Homing whisked them into the dishwasher, Luke held out his arm to Jane, and she took it readily. He credited the wine for mellowing her toward him and gave thanks for it.

They left the patio and cornered the house. There was a walking path that led in two directions.

Luke paused at the fork. "Right or left?"

"You choose."

"You've been here before." He deferred to her knowledge. "Which path has the best view of the mesas?"

"Either one," she said. "But the path on the left has a wooden park bench where we could sit and watch the moon come up."

"Sold," he said and guided her left and away from the house.

Desert noises accompanied the sound of their shoes crunching against the white gravel—the call of a night bird, the chirp of crickets, the yip of a coyote. At that last sound, she moved closer to him.

"Scared of coyotes?" he asked.

"A little," she admitted.

"They're more scared of you than you are of them." He moved his arm from her elbow to her shoulder. She didn't tense or step away.

"I'm glad you're with me," she said, and her words lit him up inside. "I wouldn't feel safe walking out here alone at night, even though the path is well marked."

"I do know my way around a wildland," he said. "I've got your back."

"Thanks." She sighed softly, her body warm and supple against his. She walked with short mincing steps. "Maybe I should have changed shoes after all."

"There's the bench." He pointed. "We're almost there."

"If it wasn't cactus country, I'd just take off my shoes."

"You want to go back..." he asked. "Or..."

"What?" she prodded.

"Would you mind if I carried you to the bench?"

"I don't want you to have to do that."

"I offered."

"We should just go back."

"It's not even ten," he said. "Far too early for bed." Once Luke had said the word, he wished he hadn't because all he could think about were beds and mattresses, and Jane stretched out on them.

"Oh, look!" She inhaled sharply as her eyes turned skyward. "It's a meteor shower!"

"That settles it," he said.

"What?"

"We're staying." He scooped her into his arms and toted her to the bench.

Laughing, she wrapped her arms around his neck and held on, and Luke felt like a superhero. He settled her on the bench and then sat beside her. They watched as falling stars streaked across the sky, one right after the other.

"Are you making rapid-fire wishes?" he asked.

"One for every star." She laughed, and the sound was so beautiful, so genuine, his heart suddenly felt too tight in his chest.

"Different wishes?" he asked. "Or the same one?"

"Different. You?"

He peered into her eyes. "Just the one."

"Ooh," she said. "What's that?"

"Can't tell you," he said. "Or it won't come true."

Another star zipped across the sky, and Luke wished for a bond with his grandfather. That's why he was here, after all. Luke didn't give two figs for the company. All he wanted was to connect with Rupert while there was still time.

"Do you want to know what I wished for?" she asked, coyly lowering her lashes and giving him a sidelong glance.

"Don't tell me if you want it to come true," he cautioned.

"You don't really believe that, do you?"

"Hey, I don't really believe falling stars grant wishes." He shrugged and winked. "But then again, who knows? Why risk it?"

"I wished you would kiss me," Jane murmured so softly he wasn't sure he'd heard her correctly.

He stared at her.

She stared back.

The alcohol, the shooting stars, their chemistry, heck maybe all three—Luke didn't know what was happening, but things between them were heating up fast.

His dad had often warned him against relationships that started too fast. That's how Pete Black had gotten mixed up with Meredith Cox, and by moving too fast, too soon, they'd both ended up regretting their impulsiveness.

But unlike his mother, Jane was not an impulsive woman.

Sitting here in the shadow of Cathedral Rock, gazing into Jane's soulful brown eyes, and lusting after her full, pillowy lips, Luke was overwhelmed. *You really don't know what you want, do you, sweetheart?*

He didn't know why Jane wanted him to kiss her. Whether it was the beauty of the red rocks surrounding them or because she simply wanted to taste him, but his body literally ached for her.

Bad idea, Black. Terrible idea.

For so many reasons, primarily among them, Jane worked for his grandfather. Could she be using their attraction to suck him into Rupert's dream of turning the company over to Luke? Was this all so she could get her promotion? Seduce Luke, keep in him Arizona to make Rupert happy?

Kissing her was a dumb thing to do.

Very dumb.

But he craved her anyway.

She sat there looking prim and proper in her bulky sweater, her legs crossed at the ankles and her spine straight. Untouchable, it seemed, except for those enticing lips that she licked and pursed.

Waiting for his kiss.

On the surface, she was buttoned up, reserved, practical, and composed. Still, those lips promised a different sort of woman underneath that cool exterior, and he couldn't wait to taste her.

Would she taste as refreshing as he suspected? Like ice water on a blisteringly hot desert day?

Hoping that she hadn't changed her mind, Luke slid his arm around the back of the bench seat and leaned in toward her until their lips were almost touching. His pulse thundered, and his abdominal muscles twitched.

"Are you sure you want that wish to come true?" he murmured.

Mutely, Jane nodded.

Was this smart? Heck no. Should he back off? Yes. Should he make a joke? Tell her that since she told him her wish, it couldn't come true? Absolutely.

He did none of those things.

Instead, he just stared into her eyes and felt the warmth of her breath on his skin.

The night had woven a spell over them. It almost felt as if he were someone else. A man he didn't know—a man who wanted things he shouldn't want. Before common sense could stifle his need, Luke pulled her into his arms and kissed her.

Boom!

Their mouths joined. Fused.

Talk about falling star magic!

He felt the kiss not just in his mouth and tongue but in his entire body. His belly stiffened, and in seconds, he was rock hard.

Jane tensed at first, knotting her hands into fists and holding them to her chest as if keeping him at bay, but then her jaw softened, and her tongue slipped out to greet his. She skimmed her cool fingertips over his heated flesh to cup her palms against his cheeks as *she* deepened the kiss.

Whoa!

Inflamed, he took the kiss deeper still, absorbing her taste—chocolate, raspberries, and brandy. He inhaled her.

Luke cradled the back of her head in his palm, holding her steady as he poured himself into that kiss.

Into *her*.

She tasted so good. Since Luke had met her at the fountain, he'd been daydreaming of this, and kissing her was far better than he'd imagined.

He was in over his head with this one, and Luke knew it. He thrilled to her softness, her scent, reveling in her dainty body pressed so hard against his. Enjoyed the crush of his chest against her breasts.

Don't trust anything that moves too fast, too soon. Luke's father's words came to him, intruding at the worst possible moment.

Luke hesitated. Just for a second, but it was enough.

Gasping, Jane pulled back, her eyes wide and her breathing shallow. "That," she whispered, "was a huge mistake."

Chapter Seven

JANE HAD TO GET CONTROL over herself and her runaway desires.

ASAP.

Dread curled up inside her stomach, but underneath that mounting anxiety was a deep, swift current of joy.

When was the last time she'd been kissed so thoroughly? Had she *ever* been kissed so thoroughly? If she had, she couldn't remember. Surely, she'd remember a kiss like this.

Fingering her lips, which felt windblown and blistered, she stared at Luke sitting beside her on the bench. A yearning unlike anything she'd ever felt knocked her over, and it was all she could do not to kiss him again.

Go for it, Kim whispered in her head. *You deserve to have a good time.*

But no. It wasn't professional, and if Luke took over his grandfather's company, he'd be her boss, and that spelled t-r-o-u-b-l-e no matter how you looked at it.

How could she be so thrown by one little kiss?

Little?

Seriously?

She wanted this man, and yet if she followed her desires, she was terrified she'd lose herself. Gathering the self-control that she'd thrown to the wind, Jane stood up. "It's time we were getting back."

"You want me to carry you back to the path?" He jumped to his feet and came toward her. Looking as if he was about to scoop her into his arms again.

"No!" she said, then regretted speaking so emphatically. It showed Luke how unnerved she was. She lowered her voice. "I mean, no, thank you. I can manage."

"I'm hot and bothered too, Jane." He held her gaze. "You're pretty fantastic."

"I'm not hot and bothered," she denied, feeling prickly.

"No? Then why do you have sweat trickling down your temple?"

She swiped the perspiration away. She was burning up and freezing all at the same time. "It's the sweater."

"Feel free to take it off."

"No."

He shrugged, and his eyes filled with mischief. "Your call."

Walking on tiptoes to keep her heels from digging into the dirt, she went ahead of him, knowing good and well he was staring at her butt. At the thought, her body flooded with heat, and she wished like hell she hadn't worn the damn sweater.

He caught up to her. "Hey, slow down. Where's the fire?"

"No fire." She stalked along with her head held high.

"Was the kiss that bad?"

No, it was that good. Jane didn't answer, just kept going.

"Jane," he said.

"What?"

"I like you, and it was never my intention to send you running scared."

"Look, I asked you to kiss me, and you did. It's not your fault. I oversaw my own behavior. Kissing you was like caviar."

"What?"

"Something I always wanted to try, but it didn't live up to the hype." She was telling the truth about caviar, but not about his kiss.

"Oh."

She'd reached the back patio where they'd had dinner. All the plates had been whisked away. It was a pleasant life, being waited on hand and foot. A life she had no business living. Stopping, she turned to him.

"You're terrified," he accused.

"I'm not terrified," she lied. "I've just got better things to do than stand around gabbing with you."

With that, she ducked inside and raced upstairs to her bedroom, where she absolutely had nothing better to do.

JANE COULDN'T SLEEP.

She tossed. She turned. She stared at the ceiling.

At two a.m., she got up and took her second shower of the night, hoping that the warm water would soothe her agitation.

It did not.

She'd no sooner gotten out of the shower, dried off, and donned her bathrobe than she heard a ragged masculine scream.

Alarm spread through her. Luke? Was he alright?

Worry pinched her. Tightening the belt on her bathrobe, Jane went into the hallway. She heard the sound again, although this time it was a guttural shout of warning and not a scream coming from the bedroom across the hall from hers.

Luke's bedroom.

Was he having a nightmare? Or was he in trouble?

She moved to his door, raised her hand, thought about knocking. Did she really want to see him bare-chested with mussed hair and a knowing grin?

Pausing, fist raised, she considered what to do.

Another scream. It sounded like Luke was in pain.

Freaked out, she tried the knob, and the door swung inward. It wasn't locked. Jane pushed it all the way open and tentatively stepped into the darkened room.

"Luke," she called. "Is something wrong?"

"No! No, no!" Luke cried out. "Don't leave me!"

Fear gripped Jane, and she bolted to his bedside. "What is it, Luke? What's wrong?"

Luke was sitting upright in bed, his eyes wide and glazed, staring sightlessly as if he'd seen a ghost.

Without giving a thought to the implications of what she was doing, Jane crawled onto the mattress beside him. She wrapped her arms around the big strong cowboy trembling so hard that his teeth chattered.

"It's all right. You're all right. It was just a bad dream." She made shushing noises, low and gentle.

"Huh?" He blinked at her as if seeing her for the first time. "Jane? What are you doing here?"

"You were yelling so loudly I could hear you from across the hall."

"I was?"

"You scared the pants off me." For the first time since coming to the room, she realized she wore only a bathrobe, and she cinched the tie tighter.

Luke let out a long sigh. "I'm sorry I alarmed you. I have these damn nightmares. I thought I was over them but apparently, coming to America triggered them..."

"Do you want to talk about it?"

He shook his head.

She leaned over to turn on the bedside lamp. "Can I get you something? Glass of water? A cool cloth for your head?"

He pressed the heels of his hands against his eyes. "No, no. I'll be fine."

"You don't seem fine," Jane fretted. "Are you sure you don't want to talk about the nightmare?"

Wincing, Luke grunted. "No."

"Okay, okay." She pressed her hands downward, feeling a little hurt but not taking his grumpiness personally. That nightmare must've been scary for easygoing Luke to react so strongly.

"You know," he said, "think I would like that ice water after all."

"Great," Jane said, relieved to have something to do. "I'll be right back."

WHY HAD HE ASKED HER for ice water? Why hadn't he just sent her back to her room? He wished she hadn't heard him crying out as he was ensnared in the recurring nightmare that had haunted him from childhood after his mother ran off and left him with his father. In the dreams, he's always five years old and trapped in a Hansel and Gretel forest and couldn't find his way out. A giant wolf was stalking him, and he started to run. He tripped over a tree root, and just as the terrifying monster was about to eat his face...

He woke up.

Luke blew out his breath. He hadn't had the dream since college. Why now?

Scratching his head, he got up and padded to the bathroom. By the time he returned, Jane was wrapping softly on his bedroom door.

"Come in."

She entered the room still wearing just the bathrobe and bunny slippers. She looked so adorable. Luke remembered their kiss underneath the shooting stars and felt his body growing hotter and harder.

"Here you go." She eased down on the end of his bed and extended the glass.

He grabbed the water and downed it. "Thanks."

"You're welcome."

"You can leave now. I'm fine."

"Did I make you angry somehow?" she asked.

Black, you're being an asshole. "No, it's not you." He ran a palm over his head.

"If you want to talk, I'm all ears." She smiled softly, and her tone was gentle.

Jane was simply too lovely to be working for a guy like his money-grubbing grandfather. He wished she hadn't gotten herself tangled up with him and his dysfunctional relative.

"Look, you're making a bigger deal of this than it is. Trust me, I'm fine."

"I had a recurring dream for many years after my parents were killed," she admitted, linking her hands and dropping them into her lap.

"Honestly, Jane, I'm not in the mood for armchair psychology. I appreciate your concerns truly, but I'm fine."

She eyed him. "You don't look fine."

He rattled the ice in the glass and set it on the bedside table. "Please, go back to bed and get some sleep. I'll see you in the morning."

"I don't mind being your sounding board if you have something you need to get off your chest."

Couldn't she take a hint? He noticed she was staring at his bare chest. All he had on were his boxer briefs, and he felt overexposed.

"Why are you hanging out with me?" he asked.

"It's my job. Your grandfather sent me here to teach you how to be a corporate CEO."

"I'm not talking about that. I mean, why are you really here in my bedroom in the middle of the night?"

They were staring at each other.

She licked her lips. "That kiss wasn't caviar. I lied because it was—"

"Monumental," he finished.

"For you too?"

"Do you have any doubts?"

"No doubts at all. As far as anything else goes? All I've got are doubts," she murmured.

"I want to kiss you again."

"I want that too."

He wasn't going to ask twice, and damn if she didn't cross the room at the same time. She wrapped her arms around his neck, and he slid his arms around her waist.

Then he kissed her, and it was even better than before.

"Oh my," she whispered against his mouth. "Oh my."

Primal emotions grabbed the center of him and twisted hard. He slipped his tongue between her teeth, and Jane let him in. Not only that, but she played her tongue over his lips, his teeth, the roof of his mouth.

Nothing in this world had ever tasted better.

There was simply no going back for either one of them.

At this moment, she was perfection, and the world was as it should be. There was just the right amount of everything. Heat. Pressure. Moisture. Adrenaline.

Luke closed his eyes and let out a groan. She pressed herself against his entire body that throbbed with need for her.

Had he *ever* felt such a burning need?

Why was this feeling so intense? Jane was a sexy woman, sure, but he'd been with many sexy women. How was she any different from the rest? Was it because he was finally ready for a quality woman? Was he simply at the right place, at the right time?

Or was there something exceptional about her?

He had no immediate answers to those questions. His body didn't need any explanations. All it needed was *her.*

Jane.

Pretty Jane.

Finally, he broke the kiss and stepped back for a good look at her.

She was peering up at him, breathing hard and fast, just as he was. "Well," she said, "are you going to stand there staring all night, or do *I* have to carry *you* to bed?"

PEELING OFF HIS BOXER shorts, he hopped onto the bed beside her, and the next thing she knew, it was all mouths and tongues and hormones.

She was completely swept off her feet. There was no other explanation for it. That was scary. What burned the hottest burned out quickest, but what was wrong with that? All she wanted was to feel good.

And boy did she feel g-o-o-d.

Her body was warm and ready for him. Honestly, she'd been ready since she'd seen him at the fountain, breaking all the rules, throwing protocol to the wind.

And that was her attraction to him. Well, besides his rocket-hot body and gorgeous face. She liked the wildness. The lonesome cowboy. The myth. The pathos. He was the secret dream she'd never known she wanted to dream.

Until now.

His fingers were calloused. No CEO hands here. Mr. Cox had instructed her to get him a haircut and manicure, but she liked his rough edges.

He was touching her in all the right places, at just the right pace. Not too slowly, not too quickly, just perfect.

Her need for him grew by the minute, swelling and urging her on. "More," she whispered. "I need more of you."

"You got it, Janie." His hands skimmed her body. Everywhere he touched, he lit her up like fire.

She tasted salty skin, savored his cowboy flavor. This was her idea of a real man. Tanned and muscular, a man who worked with his hands. Why was Rex so determined to turn him into a polished corporate guy? Why couldn't he honor Luke for who he was? Why did he feel compelled to manipulate his grandson?

She would have a talk with Rex later. Luke deserved to be accepted and respected without jumping through hoops to please his grandfather.

Jane whimpered, overcome with need.

Luke kissed his way down her body, going lower and lower until she was on fire for him and terrified that she would spontaneously combust. He didn't take her. She writhed against him, arched her back, and begged him to take her.

"Not yet, sweetheart," he whispered. "I want to savor you."

And savor he did, spending a good long time to work her up into a frenzy of pleasure. He eased her onto her side. Explored every part of her. The back of her neck, the curve of her spine, the crease at her butt and thigh. He teased her with his mouth and stroked her with his fingers, caressing and massaging her tender flesh.

His smell, uniquely Luke, masculine and pleasing, filled her nose, and she wanted to smell him for the rest of her life. She flipped over so she could sniff his hair.

"Are you smelling me?"

"Oh yeah, babe."

Babe? Had she actually called him that? Embarrassment suffused her body, momentarily putting her pleasure on pause.

But then Luke took a big sniff of her too, and they were giggling and hugging and kissing, and it was glorious.

Dizzy with sensation, she stared into his eyes and he into her. "Protection?"

"Give me a sec." He hopped off the bed and rushed to his duffel bag.

She couldn't help watching his butt flex as he walked. He dug around inside the pocket and, grinning, produced a condom. Two seconds later, he was back on the bed beside her, and they picked up where they left off.

Jane curled her fingers around him, awed by the velvety hardness of him.

He groaned at her touch.

"Make me come, Luke, please make me come."

That was all the invitation he needed.

He penetrated her, and all the air left her body on one long, happy sigh. Control shattered for them both. And they were frantic, grasping and tugging and calling each other's names. It was as if she'd lit a match and set fire to gasoline.

Faster, harder, he moved inside her, and she responded at the same tempo, the two of them like wild animals mating on the mesa.

She felt the orgasm building low in her body, growing hotter and wilder. So much pressure. She was gasping for relief. And just when she thought it would not come, she exploded. Luke soon followed, and they fell to the pillows, clutching each other in a satisfied embrace.

But the second it was over, Jane thought, *what in the world have I done?*

LUKE AWOKE A FEW HOURS later to find the mattress beside him empty. Jane had slipped out in the night, leaving him.

Alone.

Nothing new about that.

He just hadn't expected to feel so hurt by her departure. He'd a great time, and he'd thought...well, he'd thought maybe they could build on that great sex.

Apparently, Jane did not feel the same way.

How should he handle things in the morning when he saw her again? Act as if nothing had happened? Wait for her to bring it up? Get ahead of things by broaching the topic first? Play it by ear?

He reached for his cell phone, aching to text her and ask her where she went and why she'd taken off. But common sense prevailed, and he put the phone back on the nightstand. She needed space, and he had to give it to her. Obviously, things had moved too fast for her.

For him, too, if he was honest.

It had been a long time since he'd felt this way, and the last thing that he wanted was to blow it before things even got started.

After some serious tossing and turning—dang, the pillows smelled like her—Luke fell into a restless sleep.

Where he dreamed of sweet Jane in his bed, and he was making love to her all over again.

Chapter Eight

"I'M RETURNING TO PHOENIX," Jane announced to Luke the following day, passing up the breakfast buffet the housekeeper had set out. She was skipping food but latched on to a cup of strong black coffee as though it were a lifeline. "I'll call Ms. Polk and let her know so she can replace me."

Going back home was the only smart thing to do after last night. She'd slept with her boss' grandson. There was no coming back from that. It was time to kiss her promotion goodbye.

"Whoa," Luke said, tipping back his Stetson and staring down at her with a startled expression. "What's going on?"

"I blew it. Last night was a mistake. We can't continue this way."

"Why not?" He looked honestly perplexed. In his hand, he held a plate laden with eggs, bacon, hash browns, and grilled sourdough toast.

"It's unethical."

"In what way?"

"I'm supposed to be teaching you, not sleeping with you."

"I'm not a minor, and you're not my schoolteacher. I don't see the problem."

"Your grandfather is my boss."

"Still not seeing the issue."

"Office romances are problematic."

"I'm not in your office."

"No, but you will be my boss if your grandfather decides to turn over the reins of the company to you."

"That's not happening, Jane." His voice was so soothing. "I have no interest in becoming CEO of Cox Corp."

"Then why are you here?"

"I thought I'd get some quality time with my grandfather."

"That's it?"

"That's it."

She exhaled through pursed lips and said in a rush, "I still think it's best if I leave."

"And give up your chance at promotion?"

"It's for the best."

"Slow down. Let's think this through. No one has to know we slept together."

"I'll know."

He grinned wickedly, which did nothing to ease her doubts. "Me too."

"So, you see, I have to leave."

"You don't. I promise from here on out to keep my hands to myself. We'll just pretend last night never happened."

"You can do that?"

"Like falling off a log."

"You're way more than I can handle, Black. Last night was..."

Did he wince at that, or was it her imagination? Quickly, he posted up a big smile. "A bad idea."

"Yes."

"You've nothing to gain and everything to lose by running away."

"I'm not running away. I'm throwing in the towel, and I'll regain my self-respect," Jane mumbled, blowing across her coffee to keep from meeting his gaze.

"You haven't lost anything. I respect you a whole helluva lot."

"Staying is pointless. This is nothing but a game to you, but it's my job on the line."

"Okay, maybe I wasn't taking this seriously enough, but I promise I can straighten up and fly right. Give me a second chance. What do you say? One more day? If I don't mind my p's and q's, I'll help you pack."

Jane felt marginally better. Maybe she didn't have to run back to Phoenix to save her heart after all.

"We're supposed to go shopping today, right?" he said.

She nodded. "Ms. Polk made the appointment."

"I promise to be a model shopper. I'm putty in your hands. Tell me what to do, and I'll do it."

"Okay, I have a list of things you're supposed to buy."

"Courtesy of the redoubtable Ms. Polk?"

"She's very efficient."

"Where are we going shopping? Phoenix? Sedona is not exactly the hub of fashion."

"Actually, there's a very nice shopping center here in Sedona, the Plaza de la Sol. Mr. Cox gets most of his suit's tailor-made there."

"No kidding?"

"You need a proper suit...or three. I've seen your upcoming schedule. You'll need professional attire. And Mr. Cox is adamant that you get a haircut and manicure."

"Are you freaking kidding me?" He shook his head vigorously. "No way am I getting my nails done."

"I could head back to Phoenix right now..." She gestured toward the door.

He drummed his ragged nails on the tabletop. "Okay, fine, I'll get a manicure, but you have to get your nails done too, so I'll have someone to talk to besides the manicurist."

"All right." She giggled.

"You think it's funny?"

"I do. Next week, the lieutenant governor will be here and—"

"I've got a meeting with the lieutenant governor of Arizona?"

"He's good friends with your grandfather."

"Who contributes to his campaign, I'm guessing."

"Of course, he does. Your grandfather wants you to make a good impression."

"I capitulate," Luke said. "I'm yours to costume and primp for whatever charade my grandfather has planned."

"Will you actually wear the new clothes after we pick them out?"

"You're too pretty to be so cynical, Janie."

"Stop calling me that! Will you wear them?"

"I will wear whatever you—personally—lay out for me."

"All right then. We'll leave in twenty minutes. It's nine thirty-two." Jane consulted the time on her cell phone. "Finish up your breakfast, and we'll go. I'll drive."

"Aww."

"What's wrong now?

"I like to drive. Especially Granddaddy's wheels."

She gave him a no-nonsense look which he took to mean he did not get to drive the Ferrari. "Be outside in nineteen minutes. We're taking my car."

CONTROLLING THE WILD cowboy was exhausting.

The fifteen-minute drive felt like a half-day trek over uncharted territory. Her little compact was crowded with Luke scrunched into the passenger seat. Her arm brushed his every time she had to make a turn, and there was no way to avoid it without asking him to keep his hands in his lap.

But she didn't want to ask because then he'd know she was bothered by the contact.

Jane decided to act as if last night had never happened. It seemed the best policy. On the other hand, Luke was acting as if they were besties. Chatting up a storm, telling her all about his life in Africa. She was so anxious about having had sex with him she could hardly concentrate on what he was saying.

Jane found the Plaza de la Sol without any trouble, and she had a good idea where Javiar's was located, the exclusive menswear establishment where the owner himself was waiting for them.

Jane regretted having to rush past all the interesting shops and galleries featuring Southwestern arts and crafts, jewelry stores with displays of silver, turquoise, onyx, and other gemstones, the Christmas shop, a toy shop catering to the child in everyone, and a fragrant-candle boutique.

She was eager to hurry through the shady tiled plaza graced by a small fountain with water tinkling through an upraised pitcher held by a concrete cupid. It wasn't hard to imagine Luke stopping to cool his feet in the coin-littered pool surrounding it.

But she couldn't resist stopping at a glassblower's stall. The man was making a whimsical little creature, blowing through a pipe, and twisting nimbly to form a fragile swan.

"Isn't that beautiful!" she exclaimed, touching Luke's arm without thinking. Quickly, she dropped her hand. "I wish I could make something like that."

"I'll get it for you," Luke offered. "A gift to thank you for all you're doing."

"No. Thank you, anyway. I just like to watch glassblowers. When I was little, I wanted to create blown glass art. Not a very practical career goal."

"Ms. Polk definitely wouldn't approve."

"No, she probably wouldn't. Look, there's Javiar's."

The shop was located on the balcony level, sandwiched between a leather goods shop and a store that seemed to sell nothing but beads. Jane was eager to get this ordeal over with.

"Mr. Cox's assistant made an appointment for us," she told the reedy young man in a charcoal suit who greeted them as they entered the store.

"Of course, Ms. Grant," he said before she could mention her name and gave a slight bow as if she were royalty. "And Mr. Black."

The proprietor, Mr. Javiar himself, bustled out to greet them. He was small and impeccably dressed in a greenish-gray silk-blend suit. Luke would get the crown-prince treatment.

"This way, sir," Mr. Javiar said, indicating a cubicle on one side of the store. "I'll take your measurements there."

Three early-bird tourists, fifty-something women, overdressed for Arizona but probably at home in East Coast designer showrooms, were pretending to examine hand-loomed neckties. At the same time, they watched Luke saunter to the small partition. Mr. Javiar, wielding a cloth tape measure, followed, along with the reedy assistant, who carried a tablet computer.

Jane hung back, pretending to check out some silk shirts in a glass case.

"There's one I definitely would like," the plumpest of the tourists said with a dignified giggle.

Jane knew damn well the woman wasn't talking about ties.

The dressing room was too crowded to properly shut the curtain. Jane groaned inwardly when she caught a glimpse of Luke's torso, bare to the navel with a jade amulet in the shape of an arrowhead hanging on a leather cord between his spectacular pecs. One of the tourists was openly staring, slack-jawed in admiration.

"Waist thirty-three and a quarter," Mr. Javiar said crisply. "Now elevate your left arm, please, Mr. Black."

The tape flicked around Luke's hips as though it had a life of its own, and Jane annoyed herself by wondering how much room they allowed for expansion in that particular area. She knew firsthand how much room Luke needed.

Feeling her cheeks flush, Jane took a deep breath and decided that, for once, Kim was right. She did need to work on her social life. She needed a sweet, sane, reliable man to ward off fantasies about wild, untamable cowboys.

Covering her mouth to conceal a yawn as she imagined dating some nice junior executive, Jane was startled by a female shriek.

What was going on?

She jerked her head around to see Luke racing past her, an unbuttoned white business shirt clinging to his shoulders like sails on a ship.

He'd bolted!

Okay, he didn't want new clothes, but this was ridiculous. Javier scurried after him, muttering something about expensive silk. His assistant trailed behind, anxiously whipping the tape measure around his hand.

Jane stepped out on the balcony just in time to see Luke grab a vine from a plant clinging decoratively to the wrought-iron railing and leap off into space.

"Oh no!" she exclaimed and raced to peer over the balcony, expecting to see him lying in a crumpled heap on the red tiles below.

Instead, Luke was tackling a wiry bald man in a red shirt and grabbing something from him.

"He got my purse back," the tourist cried, nearly toppling over the railing herself in her excitement.

Jane grabbed the back of the woman's chartreuse-and-black flowered tunic blouse until she steadied herself. Still, the woman was too excited to notice.

"Marvel! He got it back!" The woman bounced and applauded.

Luke hauled the purse snatcher to his feet. The plaza's security guards rushed over to take charge of what turned out to be a shaved-head juvenile, as muscular as Luke but definitely not in his league.

From then on, it was the Luke Black show.

Luke was becomingly modest but still able to milk maximum admiration from the three women shoppers and the crowd that had gathered, including the pale-faced tailor's assistant. Mr. Javiar retrieved the shirt remnants but was hard-pressed to keep a stiff upper lip as his shop began to resemble backstage after a rock concert.

Jane was torn between admiring Luke's heroics and wishing the earth would swallow her up. Against her better judgment, she was impressed by his tackling of the purse snatcher but appalled by the hopelessness of trying to change him into his grandfather's—and Ms. Polk's—dream CEO.

A security guard took statements. The female tourists fawned over their hero. Half the people in the plaza seemed to be crowded into the shop, all of them babbling with excitement. Luke was grinning with that unbuttoned white shirt showing off abs of steel.

Mr. Javiar came up to her. "I never expected anything like this. Mr. Black is..." He paused and crinkled his nose. "Unconventional to say the least."

"Do you have all the measurements you need?" she asked.

"Yes, but we didn't look at fabrics...." The man seemed stricken as if he'd failed Mr. Cox in some monumental way.

"This is what Mr. Cox has requested for Luke." She handed Javiar the computer-generated list. She'd kept it hidden from Luke, hoping to order what Ms. Polk called a "suitable wardrobe" without taking all the choices from him.

"This is"—Mr. Javiar reviewed the list—"overwhelming. We need to go over styles, coordinate the accessories, consult on—"

"No, we don't. Mr. Black needs everything on this list as soon as possible. If you can't tailor everything yourself to the specifications by the timeline, we'll settle for off the rack. I trust your judgment."

"But, Ms.—"

"How long will it take?"

"Six suits, three jackets, formal wear..." Javier was tallying the list, consternation turning to a highly refined glee. "Say four weeks."

"We need it in four days."

"That's impossible! Even if I employ temporary help—"

"Charge it all to Mr. Rupert's account. He'll be very pleased if his grandson makes a good impression at a meeting with the lieutenant governor."

"Four days." His thin lips curled around his words, and he whipped out a gleaming white handkerchief—which had probably never been used for anything as mundane as wiping away sweat—and dabbed his high forehead. "I'll have to take shortcuts. Mr. Cox never wears anything off the rack. And there will have to be fittings. That's essential for the *Javiar* look."

"Use a model the same size. Mr. Black isn't particular." That was the biggest understatement of her life. "Oh, and there's one change. Add Jockey shorts to the list. Two dozen pairs, nice thick hundred percent cotton."

Luke joined her and Javiar, finally leaving his moony-eyed fans behind.

"We're done," Jane said.

"All ready?"

"Yes. Let's go."

"Okay, then." Luke nodded. "Let's hit it and get it."

She didn't dare ask what "it" was.

"Can I please buy you lunch?" Luke asked as they left the store. "I want to make up for disrupting the shopping trip."

"We can't," she explained. "Mrs. Homing is expecting us, and you have to start reading the corporate reports."

Luke groaned. "Do I have to?"

"I'm afraid so."

"You're a hard taskmaster, Jane Grant."

"Thank you for saying so."

Luke snorted, but in a friendly way.

He was quiet all the way to the car. For a moment, she thought he was going to open the door for her, then he patted the deep pockets of his Wranglers as if he was searching for lost keys, but why? She was driving.

"Forgot something," he said. "Would you mind waiting just a minute?"

"No, but—"

Watching him trot away, Jane couldn't imagine what he might have left behind, but it was a very nice view, so she refused to complain.

Chapter Nine

MRS. HOMING SERVED turkey sandwiches and potato salad for lunch, with chocolate chip cookies for dessert.

They ate poolside near the waterfall, at a small bistro table underneath the shelter of a large umbrella. Mellow music played from the sound system, and Jane recognized the soothing stylings of Jack Johnson and found her toes tapping unbidden to "Banana Pancakes."

"Watching you swing from that vine to nail that purse snatcher was pretty impressive," Jane told him.

"Turn you on, did it?" he asked with a quirky smile.

"Oh no." She couldn't help returning his grin and she waggled her finger at him. "We're not going there, cowboy. Last night was one time only."

"Can you blame me for taking a shot?" He locked eyes with her.

"You promised to behave."

He hung his head but didn't look the least bit ashamed.

"I don't want to leave, but if you keep that up, I'll be forced to go," Jane warned.

He sobered quickly and raised both palms. "No more innuendo."

"Thank you."

"Is it bad that I want to kiss you again?"

"Black!"

"Okay, okay." Laughing, he ducked and covered his head.

"Straighten up." She swatted his shoulder lightly. "Department heads will be here tomorrow to start your meetings. No more teasing."

"Not even when we're alone?"

Jane pointed at the security camera under the eaves. "We're never really alone here."

Luke eyed the camera and mumbled something under his breath that she couldn't quite make out.

Jane yawned and tried to hide it with her hand. Between the turkey, the music, and the lack of sleep last night, she was pooped.

"Hey, why don't you go take a nap?" Luke invited, standing to gather up their plates.

She shook her head. "I've got to help you prep for the meetings tomorrow."

"Nap, Janie. You want to be at your best when my grandfather's contingency shows up."

He was right about that.

"You don't mind?"

"Not at all."

"Go ahead and look through the documents Ms. Polk put together for you," she said. "It'll make our discussion of the topics covered easier."

"Yeah, yeah, sure, sure." Balancing the plates, he waited for her to rush ahead to open the door for him as he carried the dishes to Mrs. Homing in the kitchen. "Now go to bed."

She yawned again. "I don't know if I should."

"You want me to take a nap with you, Janie?"

"If I'm napping, then I am doing it solo."

"Worth a shot." He grinned.

A third yawn overtook her. "Maybe just twenty minutes."

"Sweet dreams." He winked.

Jane rolled her eyes, but inside her belly, a fire was lit. Damn him.

Her air-conditioned room was deliciously cool after the heat on the patio. She slipped off her shoes and started to turn back the heavy ivory bedspread when she saw something on the pillow.

A small black box with gold lettering on the cover.

Almost as puzzled as she was curious, she lifted the lid and took out a small object wrapped in tissue to find the exquisite handblown glass swan in her palm.

Luke had given her a present. That's why he'd gone back into the shopping center without her.

"Oh, Mr. Black," she whispered, tracing the delicate bird with her finger. "You really shouldn't have."

TWO HOURS LATER, DROWSY from her nap and searching for a hit of caffeine to shake off her slumber, Jane walked unnoticed into the kitchen as Mrs. Homing stood, shaking a furious finger at Luke.

"Get those filthy things out of my kitchen!"

"They can't hurt you," Luke said, looking as dumbfounded as Jane felt. "They're just the—"

"I know what they are, and I draw the line at having such things in my kitchen. Get them out!"

"Get what out?" Jane asked, half expecting to see tarantulas scurrying across the floor, her worst-case scenario.

"While you were napping, I decided to repair a section of downed fence I saw while we were star watching last night, and after I finished, I found a dead rattlesnake," Luke explained. "I have a friend in Botswana who'd give his eyeteeth for rattles like these." He held out his hand to let her inspect his trophy. "I had no idea anyone would object. There's no poison in the tail."

Mrs. Homing held a rolling pin as if it were a baseball bat but managed to speak more calmly. "Your weird ways are your business, I'm sure, but I'm terrified of snakes. I want no part of one round me."

"I'm sorry, ma'am. Won't happen again." Luke tipped his Stetson to her. "I'm no hunter anyway. I believe all creatures have a right to stay in their natural environment." He gave Jane a penetrating look she chose to ignore.

She wasn't going to leap to his defense; she didn't like his grisly souvenirs any better than the housekeeper did.

"A man has to know where he belongs, too," he said in a low voice just loud enough for Jane to hear.

"You belong out on the patio so we can go over the documents you read while I was napping."

Luke winced. "About that..."

"You didn't read them."

"The fence needed repairing."

"An excuse."

"Maybe."

"Well, it doesn't matter," she said efficiently. "I can fill you in between now and dinner."

"About that..."

"What?"

"I called an old friend who lives in Scottsdale now, and he asked me to dinner."

"I see."

"I'd invite you along, but we intend on getting plastered. We haven't seen each other since college."

"Bye," she said, waving him away. "Go."

"Thanks, Janie." He leaned over, kissed the top of her head, and was gone before she could react.

"He's unexpected, that one," Mrs. Homing said and poured Jane a tall glass of iced tea. "Half the time you want to pinch his cheeks, and the other half you want to kick his backside."

"Indeed." Jane sighed, took her iced tea, and escaped to the pool.

Before sitting, Jane checked the chair cushions, potted plants, and the ground around the table. She was a native of Arizona; she knew there were creatures that she'd rather not confront. Leave it to Luke to shatter the imaginary line between "out there" and "in here."

Unfortunately, that wasn't the only image he was shattering.

THE MORNING SUN STREAMING through the windows did nothing to improve Luke's sense of loneliness. There hadn't been a friend in Scottsdale. He'd made it all up so he wouldn't have to hear Janie lecture him about corporate policy when all he wanted to do was take her to bed.

Instead of whooping it up at a bar, he'd gone on a desert hike. Yesterday's climb hadn't been steep enough, nor the terrain rugged enough, to clear his mind the way he'd hoped. One day of exploring hadn't provided him any more insight into his grandfather or what to do about his budding feelings for Jane.

The hike had been dangerous. Not physically, of course—Luke could handle that kind of challenge. The real peril came from letting Jane inside his head. His gut feeling was that Rupert was using her as bait to keep him in the country permanently. Central question: Was the old man doing it with or without her knowledge?

He finished dressing, pulling on his hiking boots for another day trekking around the ranch until the suits showed up for their meetings. No doubt Ms. Polk had prepared a schedule for him to follow, but she—make that Rupert—wasn't going to pull his strings. If Rupert had things to tell him, let him do it in person. He might be ailing, but Luke wasn't going to let him use his health condition to manipulate. Somehow Luke had gotten the impression when he'd first arrived that he'd be spending the thirty days getting to know his grandfather, not being groomed by strangers for a job he didn't want.

Honestly, his feelings were hurt.

What was this stay in Sedona about? Some kind of initiation rite Rupert had engineered to make him worthy of running the company? Luke had no intention of jumping through hoops for anyone, not even a grandfather. He was tempted to call the whole visit off. Rupert had never been there for him. Why did he have to be there for his grandfather now that the old coot was sickly?

If it weren't for Jane, he'd leave, but then she wouldn't get her promotion, and he couldn't bring himself to mess her over like that.

"Janie, love," he muttered under his breath, "you've certainly complicated things."

AFTER LUKE LEFT, JANE did a bit of work, set her alarm for the crack of dawn, and went to bed. She managed to get downstairs, carrying the paperwork she and Luke were set to discuss, even before Mrs. Homing arrived.

She started the coffee, made toast from a loaf of whole wheat, and smeared it with honey and peanut butter. No skipping breakfast today. She was going to need fuel for maximum energy. No way was Luke Black going to evade his responsibilities today. She'd slathered on sunscreen and dressed in denim shorts, running shoes, a short-sleeved blue oxford-cloth shirt, and a cotton baseball cap. Wherever he tried to go, she would follow.

"You're up early, Ms. Grant."

"Eep!" Jane startled and clutched her chest. Luke had crept unnoticed into the kitchen.

"Sorry," he apologized. "I didn't mean to scare you."

"I didn't know you were up yet." She made sure her tone said she wasn't in the mood for his nonsense.

"Don't know that I've ever had honey like that." He poked his finger into the jar of spun honey and sucked it with appreciative noises.

She moved the honey out of his immediate reach. "It's not nice to stick your fingers into communal food. Other people use this honey too. Would you like some toast?"

"Three or four eggs lightly over and four slices of bacon would be great," he said, sitting on one of the plank-seat chairs beside a long, bleached wood table.

"I'm not..." She started to say, "the cook," but decided it would be a good idea to feed him. She could talk about what he was supposed to do while he was occupied with breakfast. "I'm not very good at fried eggs. I usually break the yolks."

"No problem." He locked his hands behind his head and stretched out his long, muscular legs shod in his hiking shoes again.

The breakfast turned out to be one of her better culinary efforts: four perfect eggs, the edges brown from the bacon drippings she used to fry them, a plate of crisp, thin-sliced bacon, coffee that tasted almost as good as it smelled, and a tall glass of home-squeezed orange juice that Mrs. Homing had left in a pitcher in the fridge.

"You cook as good as you look, Janie," Luke said, munching a piece of bacon he'd picked up with his fingers and dipped in the egg yolk.

"Please use a fork when your grandfather's people get here," she begged.

He looked up, grinned, and picked up the utensil in question.

"Thank you."

"You're right, Janie. It's boorish of me. You certainly are one of Rupert's people."

"I didn't mean *me*." She reached over, snatched a strip of bacon from his plate with her fingers, and munched it. Why should she be stuck trying to teach him manners he should have learned from his mother?

Then she remembered his mom had died when he was young, and she felt a sense of immense sadness for him, knowing how she still missed her mother.

"About today, it's urgent you at least look at these reports before any company execs get here." She pushed the thick folder in his direction.

He flicked open the cover and shuffled through the papers, continuing to eat. "They look pretty dry. Will there be a quiz?"

"I wouldn't be surprised if Ms. Polk stays up all night writing one," she joked. "But remember, if you flunk, I flunk, too."

"Hardly seems fair to you." He rested his arms on the table and gazed at her.

"It's business," she said weakly, looking down at her empty coffee cup. "You know, no one is making you go through with this. If you don't intend to go into your grandfather's business, why bother staying here?"

Why make me stay here, she implied with her eyes.

"He's my only relative. He's got a heart condition, and I'd thought he might show up at his ranch, and we could hang out."

"Maybe he will show up," she offered to give him hope.

"I have questions for him, but I won't find the answers in this." He pushed the folder away.

"Maybe let's just go over this for an hour—"

"I've taken a fancy to the red rocks. There's a trail I want to follow...."

"Then I'm going with you."

"Isn't that taking your responsibilities a little too seriously?"

"We'll pack a lunch. You can look through these then." She pushed the pages back toward him.

"You're so set on this paperwork that you'd trail-hike with me in the blazing sun?"

"I'll wear a hat and sunscreen and bring plenty of water. Don't think for one minute I can't keep up."

"You couldn't keep up if I had a mind to leave you behind." He shrugged, not exactly a show of enthusiasm.

Mrs. Homing came in then, still a little cool toward Luke for bringing the snake rattles into her kitchen the day before but willing enough to put together a picnic for them.

> "Meet me by the front door in twenty minutes," Luke said.

"How do I know you won't leave without me?"

"Janie, you've got to stop being so skeptical. If I say I'll do something, I do it. Eventually. I give you my word. I'll wait."

She believed him. Whatever character flaws he had, dishonesty didn't seem to be one of them.

True to his word, he was waiting for her twenty minutes later, an old khaki backpack sitting on the floor by the main entrance.

"Borrowed it from Willard," he said. "If you're dead set on lugging those papers, you can stick them in my kit. You'll have your work cut out for you just keeping up without carrying a load."

"I belonged to the hiking club in high school," she said, miffed by his assumption that she wasn't up to the challenge. "We went on field trips in the mountains and down into the Grand Canyon. You won't have to slow down for me."

His grin was aggravating. If this cowpoke thought he had a monopoly on stamina, he'd better enjoy eating her dust.

AFTER SEVERAL HOURS of hiking, Jane was still keeping up. She had spunk. Luke had to give her that. He'd gotten the lay of the land yesterday afternoon while she napped, and he'd deliberately picked a route that involved the most excellent uphill hiking. Part of him wanted her to beg off when the going was rough. Unfortunately, his feelings about her were so mixed, and he was enjoying her company immensely.

She was witty when she wasn't worried about answering to Ms. Polk, energetic enough to keep up with him, and so beautiful with her dark hair tied in a ponytail and bobbing out from under her little hat that he found himself inventing reasons to take her hand or guide her by the arm or fall back and watch the way her calves and buttocks flexed when she climbed.

Worse, he let his imagination run amok, looking for flat rocks and level areas where they could—

Where nothing was going to happen because he was leaving and going back to his natural environment, one time was a casual hookup. If he had sex with Jane again, that was a trend. A trend he shouldn't count.

A man could lose his heart to beauty—in the wilderness of Arizona or the eyes of a beautiful woman—but Luke couldn't let either become a snare.

Chapter Ten

HER CALVES WERE TIGHT and achy. Keeping up with Luke was no leisurely stroll, and she hadn't done any serious hiking in quite a while. Jane could handle the discomfort. Pride alone would carry her along on that score. What was really uncomfortable was being near Luke and having to keep her hands off him.

He was so gorgeous. His body was incredible. Yes, he was impulsive and could act a little rashly at times, but honestly, she saw that as a childlike curiosity in the world around him. He was so present with the environment. So knowledgeable. Stopping to point out plants and teach her ways to survive if she ever found herself lost in the desert without water.

Sure, he wasn't an ideal candidate for the corporate milieu, but he was creative and spontaneous and just plain fun.

Here was the sticking point. Luke wanted more from her than that one-time hookup. She saw it in the way he leveled sidelong glances at her or took her hand to boost her up a rock.

And there was that swan.

The beautiful blown glass swan.

A sweet and thoughtful gift. That was the action of someone who wanted more, whether Luke would admit it or not.

Ack! She was driving herself bonkers.

Jane ached to get closer to him. What was under his sometimes breezy, sometimes brash exterior? Was he genuinely indifferent to his grandfather's company and money? Or was it all an act for some reason that escaped her? Was she a fool, reading more into his character than was sensible? Maybe that was it. Her track record with men was abysmal. Dead-end relationships were her specialty.

"Are you okay?" He turned and offered his hand again to help her up a steep incline.

"Just fine, thank you."

His fingers were long and hard, gripping her wrist with easy pressure. She loved strong hands, especially when they were gentle.

"There's a plateau up ahead, a good place for a rest if you're ready for lunch."

"If you're hungry..." She didn't want him to stop because he thought she needed to rest.

"I'm always hungry." He said it in a way that suggested he was talking about more than just food.

"All right, we'll stop, then."

The sunbaked, rocky ground was too hot for comfort, but Luke found a small patch of shade and spread out a checkered cloth. Sitting side by side with his hip wedged against hers, they could hardly avoid touching. They wolfed down ham sandwiches, potato chips, and more of those chocolate chip cookies, all washed down with a thermos of iced tea.

"Do you mind if I stretch out and relax in the sun for a bit?" he asked. "Rest does wonders for the stamina."

She eyed him, suspicious that he wanted to slow down for her. "I was hoping you'll look through some of these documents while we're resting."

Ms. Polk's dreary reports seemed trivial compared to the vivid burnt-orange rock formations and the limitless azure canopy of the sky. She wished her job wasn't in jeopardy, prompting her to act like Ms. Polk's go, go, go clone.

"Give me ten minutes, and I'll give them my full attention," he drawled. Sleepily, he stretched out on his back, pulled the straw Stetson down over his face, and was either asleep instantly or pretending to be.

She looked at her watch, realizing she had to stay awake to time his nap, or they both might suffer from bad sunburns despite their slathering of sunscreen.

Minutes passed.

Her lids grew heavy. She couldn't imagine anything more pleasant than cushioning her head on his chest and dropping off to sleep.

The heat was fast sapping the last of her energy. Twice her eyes shut, her head bobbing forward as she tried to stay awake. She curled up, using Luke's shoulder as a pillow, not intending to sleep, only rest for a minute.

What was that saying about good intentions?

"WAKE UP, SLEEPYHEAD."

"Huh?" Jane woke with a start, realizing what she'd done. She sat up blinking. Yawning and stretching, she peered at him. "How long was I asleep?"

"Only a few minutes. Just the thing to recharge your batteries."

She crawled over to the backpack on her hands and knees and drank from her water bottle. Yawning again, she pulled the paperwork from the pack. "Here we go."

He grimaced. "You're not going to hold me to a work schedule and make me read this right now, are you?"

"The sales force arrives tomorrow. The next day you'll meet the plant manager and—"

"Right. What happened with the lieutenant governor?"

"That got canceled."

"Thank heavens." He pantomimed wiping sweat off his forehead in relief.

"So read." She thrust the papers at him.

He handled the document with the same disdain Mrs. Homing had for snake rattles. Pushing his sunglasses up on the bridge of his nose, he read a line or two. "None of this has anything to do with me."

He tossed the papers back toward her, but a gust of wind caught the sheaf and floated the documents to the path they'd taken to get up here.

"I'll get them." She scrambled down, not worrying about the steepness of the incline in her eagerness.

Luke called after her, "Jane, let it go. Let me—"

Her left foot started sliding, throwing her onto her back. She couldn't dig her heels into sheer rock, and there was nothing to grasp, no way to stop her downward plunge. She cried out, knowing there was a drop-off below the path, momentum flinging her toward the fall.

The sun was blinding, and she couldn't see any way to save herself.

Suddenly, Luke's shadow darkened her view as he leaped past her, and she tumbled into his arms. He braced her against him, his body a barrier between her and the edge of the cliff.

"Oh, Luke. Oh!"

"You're okay. Not even a close call. Easy now."

His arms tightened around her, her cheek pressed against his shoulder, her legs too shaky to support her weight. Her heart was racing, but it wasn't all from fear. She wrapped her arms around Luke's waist, unabashedly clinging, appreciating the feel of his legs hard against hers and his sunbaked cheek resting on her forehead. Sometime soon, she was going to start hurting, her back and legs bruised by the fall, but for the moment, she was engulfed by pleasure, loving where she ended up.

"I've got you," he murmured.

He tipped Jane's chin, brushing his lips across her forehead, then stood so still she could feel the beating of his heart. His lips moved slowly down to the tip of her nose, then pressed against the sensitive bow above her lips. She flattened her hands against his back, wanting him close, wanting more...

His kiss was so gentle, she was almost afraid she imagined it. His lips grazed hers like the tickling of a feather, then he stepped back, effortlessly breaking her hold on his waist and putting an arm's length between them.

"You gave me a scare." He sounded worried.

"Me, too. Sorry."

"My fault. I shouldn't have let you bring the damn reports. I had no intention of reading them. Ms. Polk can..." He took a deep breath. "Maybe we should head back."

She nodded, but she wasn't at all eager to leave this enchanted place. Nor stop being held in the arms of this enchanting man.

WHAT WAS IT ABOUT HIS kiss that made everything seem upside down and wrong side out? Jane sat on the edge of her bed, digging her bare toes into the plush carpeting, and tried to analyze how she felt about facing Luke over breakfast this morning.

Dread? No, not that, even though she was sometimes guilty of letting him intimidate her. Embarrassment? Be serious.

Yesterday afternoon, when they returned from the hike, he'd mumbled something and taken off again, and he hadn't shown up for dinner. Jane was so overwhelmed by him and confused, she hadn't even tried to find out where he went.

But she couldn't stop thinking about that kiss—or the night they'd made love. What was going on with him? What was he thinking? Was he as rattled as she? She considered bringing up the topic of their sexcapade and squelched the idea. What if she imagined things? What if he wasn't feeling some of the jumbled-up emotions charging through her?

That's why she wouldn't broach the conversation with him. She didn't want to get egg on her face to find out he wasn't developing feelings for her the way she was for him.

She was tempted to skip breakfast and hole up in her room until he went off somewhere to entertain himself.

Not one of her better ideas! The first contingent of company execs would arrive this evening, and she wasn't—*Luke* wasn't—ready for them. The tailor had promised to deliver at least one presentable outfit by this afternoon. However, she still had to get Luke to a barber and manicurist and coach him on what his grandfather expected of him in these meetings. She'd slacked off on her job, and Luke would be the one to suffer if he wasn't presentable. Who was she kidding?

This wasn't just about her job anymore. Luke was getting inside her head, wreaking havoc with her emotions. All she had to do was close her eyes to remember the pleasing scent of his sunbaked skin or feel the tickle of his breath on her eyelids or the scratch of his beard stubble against her cheek.

In a month, he'd either be back in Africa finding more solutions to food insecurities or installed in the company as the new CEO. Neither option was desirable. How could she work for him when she was smitten? Alternatively, how could she invest in him emotionally when she knew he'd be hightailing it back to Africa?

They'd had sex one time. It had been great, but it was over. Best to accept it and not keep trying to build a fairy tale out of it.

She might as well try to do her job and save her career, such as it was. Even though she had a better chance of producing a pink-striped giraffe by the sales meeting tonight than a slicked-up, civilized Luke.

Groaning aloud, she forced herself out of bed and into the new day.

LUKE BELIEVED IN KEEPING his word, but his promise to stay thirty days on this desert ranch was more taxing than he could have imagined. Rupert had baited his trap well. Jane was definitely getting under his skin.

If he had any sense at all, he'd be on the next plane out. His plans didn't include falling for a gorgeous woman, and he didn't want any more complications in his life.

His grandfather was supposed to arrive in Sedona this evening with some of his minions. Maybe the two of them would have a chance to talk about something besides sporting equipment.

An honest conversation about life and death and...the importance of family.

Or maybe not.

Was he making a big mistake, trying to get closer to his distant, withholding grandfather? He'd gotten along just fine for his entire life without this particular family tie.

Maybe he should have left things as they were. He'd waited too long to get acquainted with his grandfather. Still, before his father's death, it had seemed disloyal to seek out the man who'd vehemently opposed his parents' marriage and never tried to see him.

Luke walked naked to the oversized dresser in his room and pulled open the top drawer, amused again by the stacks of pristine white boxer briefs his little keeper had ordered for him.

When it came to clothing, his philosophy was simple: less is best. But since Jane was so set on containing his male parts in a sheath of Pima cotton, he might as well have some fun obliging her. And in the process annoy her enough to make her forget about his serious slip. Kissing her again after he'd sworn off any more sexual contact with her.

When she'd fallen, his common sense took a header over the cliff. He could still smell the flowery fragrance of her hair and taste the sweetness of her mouth. He should have made love to her then and there and gotten her entirely out of his system, but he'd been afraid—yes, that was the word, afraid.

He was already infatuated. He might totally lose it if they had sex again. One time was a fling. Twice? Well, that was a slippery slope, pun intended.

He had to put distance between them and irritating her seemed the surest method. He slipped into a pair of new underwear and a pair of jeans before padding barefooted and bare-chested down to breakfast.

"Morning, Janie," he greeted her in a teasing tone that just slipped out.

She stood staring out the dining room window at the mesas, a cup of coffee in her hand. She turned and froze. Her eyes widened as she took in his chest.

Gotcha.

"Good morning," she said stiffly and averted her eyes. "Mrs. Homing is making blueberry muffins. They'll be ready in a bit, just enough time for you to finish getting dressed."

She was playing it cool. Luke liked that, but he was counting on his outrageous behavior to make her forget his blunder on the hiking path when he'd kissed her.

He sat at the far end of the table, ignoring her suggestion to put on a shirt and watching intently while she sat on a chair as far from him as possible.

"There was a fax." Her tone was chilly enough to give him goosebumps. "Your grandfather is tied up with an important account and won't be arriving at the ranch this evening as planned."

Luke couldn't figure out how if his grandfather was still so active in the business, why did he want Luke to take over?

"The others are still coming, though, so you do *have* to study the reports today," she said. "No excuses and Ms. Polk is livid that you haven't gotten a haircut and manicure yet."

"Why did you tell her?"

"She asked, and I make it a policy to avoid lying to my boss."

"It's really none of her business," Luke muttered, but his anger was really focused on his self-important grandfather. Was it really so hard to pick up the phone and call him?

Hey, you didn't call him either. Cuts both ways.

"I'm sorry you're disappointed that your grandfather can't come," Jane said.

"No skin off my hide." He tried to act casual, but in his haste, he knocked over his chair. So much for playing it cool.

"He has a lot of responsibilities," Jane said, making a weak stab at defending her employer. "Why don't you give him a call?"

"Not interested." He stalked away, feeling ludicrous, being bare-chested and embarrassed by his dumb stunt to unnerve her.

"Luke, please don't freeze him out. He's in poor health."

"So, I'm just supposed to forgive him for treating me like crap for thirty years?"

"No, just try to bridge the gap. Could you?"

"I can't," he said. "Not right now. I'm afraid I'll say something I can't take back."

"I understand." An uneasy smile twitched at her lips.

Jane showed real class, considering his boorish behavior, but he couldn't stomach listening to her make excuses for Rupert. And damn if he'd get his hair cut or a manicure. What was she planning to do, play Delilah to his Samson? He imagined Jane chasing him with barber's shears, but it wasn't enough to restore his good humor.

He walked past the landline in the living room just as it let out a shrill peal. No way was he going to answer it. There was no one on this continent he wanted to talk to right now beyond Jane.

She caught it on the fourth ring, but he was halfway up the spiral steps by then. Intending to dump the whole pile of lily-white undies on Willard and let the caretaker keep or dispose of them. He'd had enough of Ms. Jane Grant trying to dress him like a corporate stooge.

He only half heard what she was saying on the phone, but it didn't seem to be a business call. There was concern in her voice, and he only had to hear a few sentences to know something terrible had happened.

"Are you telling me everything?" she asked, an edge of panic in her voice. "No—yes—well, call me the minute you're through with the doctor."

"What's wrong?" Luke called down.

"My sister is in the emergency department. She tried me on my cell phone, but I'd left it in my room. Thank heavens I gave her the number to the ranch landline."

"What happened?"

Jane shook her head. "I'm more worried about what she didn't tell me than what she did. She said she fell rock climbing."

"Wow. Just like you did yesterday. You two are weirdly in sync. How is your sister doing?"

"She says it's only her ankle, but—" She sank her teeth into her bottom lip and curled her hands into fists. "What if she's just saying that because she doesn't want to bother me?"

"I'll take you to her. Give me two minutes to put on a shirt. I'll be right back. Grab those damn papers too. I'll look at them when we get to the hospital."

"Really?" She stared at him as if he was her hero on a white horse.

"Absolutely."

"Thank you." She looked so relieved at his gallant offer; Luke felt his chest puff up with pride.

Pulse pounding, he raced upstairs, his petulant concerns forgotten. All that mattered now was getting Janie to her sister as soon as possible.

Chapter Eleven

IN FIVE MINUTES, LUKE had the Ferrari pulled out, and the engine revving as Jane climbed into the passenger seat.

"I really shouldn't leave the ranch," Jane fretted. "Kim's injury is probably nothing major, but I won't stop worrying until I see her."

"We'll be there in no time. Leave it to me, Janie, and hold on tight."

He didn't burn rubber pulling out of the driveway, but Jane left her stomach hit her spine as he barreled down the twisting roads.

"You don't have to speed," she said, tight-lipped and anxious.

She was a hypocrite, she knew, admonishing him for driving too fast when she loved the way the sleek sports car hugged the highway. Her pulse raced as the wind whipped hair around her face, making her feel like a kid on a carnival ride. She distracted herself from her fears about Kim, focusing instead on Luke's long legs and powerful arms as he masterfully guided the vehicle.

They didn't talk much. Occasionally, Luke would reach over to briefly cover Jane's hand with his and offer a reassuring smile.

"You're such a good driver," she said. "Even at this clip, I feel safe with you behind the wheel."

"I've driven professionally," he admitted. "For a short time in my misspent youth. I'm glad that skill is finally coming in handy."

She didn't need reassurances about his driving. He was the only man she'd met who made an automobile seem like an extension of his own body. She wanted to blame the insistent tingle running through her on the situation, but she couldn't gaslight herself. Riding beside him in the convertible was a turn-on.

By the time they left the mesas behind and hit the flat desert north of Phoenix, the Ferrari was chewing up the landscape and flouting Arizona's liberal speed limit. She expected to hear a siren behind them, but the man led a charmed life.

"Why did you quit racing?" she shouted over the wind.

"I wanted something more concrete to show for my life than prize money and trophies. When I bring agricultural solutions to a village that will feed people for generations, I get a sense of satisfaction I can't get anywhere else.

She was beginning to understand why he'd never be satisfied in a business that made recreational equipment. He'd given her something to think about besides Kim's rock-climbing accident. Still, once they were close to Mercy Hospital, the frustration of crawling through Phoenix's urban traffic intensified her anxiety.

It was just like Kim to make light of some horrendous injury. Just the fact that she'd bothered to call at all meant it could be severe.

Luke dropped her off at the emergency room entrance. "I'll park the car and then join you."

"Thanks." Waving to him, Jane walked through the pneumatic door. She approached a pink-faced Rubenesque woman in blue scrubs and a large-faced Mickey Mouse watch on her wrist, sitting behind the reception desk.

The woman glanced up with a welcoming smile. "May I help you?"

"My sister is here. Kim Grant. She fell rock climbing."

"We see a lot of that in this area," the woman said. "Beats me why anyone wants to climb a sheer rock to get nowhere. I'd be scared to death of scorpions—snakes, too, but I loathe scorpions. My uncle was bitten once. I remember him telling us kids—"

"Can I see my sister?" Jane interrupted, not wanting to be rude but desperate to see Kim.

"Go right on back." The woman gestured. "Someone will point you to the right bay."

She didn't need help locating the partly curtained cubicle where Kim was lying on a gurney with her left leg in a cast. Her sister told an animated version of her life history to a lanky young man with a tablet computer in his hand and a stethoscope around his neck.

Kim was batting her eyelashes and giving the guy a come-hither smile.

Seriously? Kim was flirting? Didn't she know it was unethical for medical personnel to date their patients? Just like it was unethical for a CEO to date an underling.

Obviously not because Kim said, "If you're not busy next Saturday, would you like to go to a concert with me?"

The guy chuckled. "There won't be any concerts in your immediate future, Ms. Grant."

Jane coughed.

"Oh, hello." Kim trained her grin on Jane. "This is my big sister, Jane. Jane meet Dr. Tom. He's a resident here, and he's single."

"Hi," Jane said to the intern.

He nodded in return.

"What happened exactly? Are you in a lot of pain?" Jane went to her sister's side.

"Not since Dr. Tom gave me a pain shot." Kim winked at the resident.

"You hurt yourself seriously?" Jane futzed with the sheets, pulling them up to her sister's chest, smoothing out the wrinkles.

"I'll give you two some privacy," Dr. Tom said and left the room.

"Jake said it was an easy climb," Kim said. "Ha!"

"Who's Jake?'

"Some guy I've dated a couple of times."

"Why were you climbing so early in the morning? Dawn isn't your style." It was only ten a.m. now. For Kim to sustain an injury, arrive at the hospital, and get the cast, she had to have been hiking at dawn.

"To tell the truth, I fell yesterday afternoon, but I didn't want to spoil things for the other campers with us. I toughed it out, took some aspirins from the first aid kit, and Jake wrapped my ankle. But it hurt so much I couldn't sleep. We left the campsite around four a.m., and Jake brought me here."

"Where's Jake now?"

"He went back for our camping gear."

"You should've come to the hospital right after it happened," Jane scolded.

"Well, Dr. Tom said it's just a simple fracture, but I'll have to wear this cast and use crutches for six weeks, and it's going to hurt a lot after the shot wears off."

Jane winced. "I'm so sorry you're hurting."

"Why can't they give shots in a more dignified place?" Kim complained.

"They have to give them where there's padding," Jane teased.

"Are you saying I have a big butt?" Kim pantomimed, throwing her pillow at Jane. "I told you there was no need to come, but I am glad to see you."

"You told me practically nothing, and I've been worried sick. Luke drove like a maniac to get me here."

"The naked cowboy is with you?" Kim's grin lit up her face. "I'm dying to meet your wild man. Bring him in."

"Forget him. Concentrate on getting well. Do you have to stay overnight?"

"Nope. They're about to discharge me. A nurse is bringing a prescription for pain pills and the crutches."

"Is your friend coming back?" Jane glanced over her shoulder.

"He might come back, but he's not exactly Mr. Reliable, so maybe not. You didn't see him, did you? Big shoulders, thick neck. He played football for ASU until he flunked out. No matter. He's history, anyway. He bitched the whole way to the hospital because he didn't get any sleep, and I don't want a guy who thinks I'm an inconvenience. I'd rather leave in case

Jake does come back. Tell me all about the sexy cowboy you're tasked with turning into a corporate drone."

"Ahem, I'm a corporate drone."

"I didn't mean it like that. You're made for regulations and routine." Kim waved a hand. "Luke, on the other hand, sounds like that environment would be his death sentence."

What could Jane say about Luke? He was an incorrigible, maddening, impossible man. And he made her insides melt, and she knew without a doubt he would not whine if she asked him to drive her to the hospital at four in the morning. In fact, she was pretty sure he'd carry her the whole way if he had to.

"Luke showed up for breakfast without a shirt on," Jane said, giving her a tidbit. "I think he was testing me."

"Wow!" Kim sat up taller in the bed. "Tell me more."

"He doesn't like me riding herd on him. I don't care for it myself, but a job is a job."

"Speaking of jobs, I'm just sick that I won't be able to work for several weeks. I can get to class all right on crutches, but no way can I wait tables just yet. Jane, I'm so sorry to put all the responsibility back on you."

"Don't worry. We'll get by. I'll get my things from the ranch, call Ms. Polk to explain what's happened, and come home to take care of you."

"You will do no such thing. I'll be perfectly fine alone. You know I'm good on crutches. It would be a tragedy if you lost your promotion because of me. Anyway, Melinda said she'd stay with me for a few days until the worst of the pain passes."

Dr. Tom returned with the prescription, crutches, and a nurse pushing a wheelchair. He offered lots of soothing advice.

While the doctor gave her discharge instructions, Jane went looking for Luke.

She found him sitting in a corner of the waiting room, a pair of gold wire-rimmed reading glasses perched on his nose as he poured over the printouts that she'd been trying to get him to read for the last four days. She'd never seen him in glasses, and the contrast between his scholarly concentration and sinewy, suntanned muscles rocked her in unexpectedly sexy ways.

Just then, the nurse wheeled Kim into the waiting room behind her. "We're ready for you to bring the car around."

"Luke," Jane introduced him. "This is my sister, Kim. Kim, this is Luke Black, Mr. Cox's grandson."

Luke set down the documents and stood, smiling like a movie heartthrob. He came over to shake Kim's hand. "Nice to meet you, Kim."

"My pleasure," her sister said, glancing sideways at Jane and winking.

Jane ignored that and gave him a quick rundown on Kim's condition. "Since you and I came in the sports car, Kim and I will take an Uber home. You can follow us." She gave him their address, and a thought stuck in her head. *Now he'll know where I live.*

"Sounds good. I'll give you an hour to get settled in," Luke said. "Then I'll swing by to pick you up. If you need more time, let me know."

"What'll you do in the meanwhile?"

He gestured toward the documents. "Finish *that* obnoxious chore."

"Thank you." Jane smiled her gratitude.

He lifted one corner of his mouth in a lopsided grin and tipped his Stetson. "See you later, gator." And then he scooped up the paperwork and headed out the door.

"LUKE'S THE ONE," KIM said when they were settled into the Uber van.

"He's too old for you, pumpkin."

"Not me, goofy. *You.* Go for it, Jane. Lasso that cowboy."

"Stop matchmaking."

"There's sparks there. I saw it with my own two eyes. Luke likes you."

"I like him too."

"So, what's the problem. Nail that *thing down.*"

"It's not that simple."

"Why not?" Kim was only nineteen. There was so much about life she didn't yet understand.

"Luke is either going back to Africa after this or taking over as CEO of the company. Either way, there's nothing there for us. Long-distance relationships don't work, nor do workplace romances. Not in the twenty-first century. Can you imagine the HR nightmare if he did become CEO and we decided to date?"

"So quit the job. You've always wanted to travel. If Luke goes back to Africa, go with him."

"He'll be living in base camps out in the jungle or the bush or whatever, and I'm used to my creature comforts. It's not the life for me. I have to be an adult about this and not start spinning fantasies. Besides, I've known him for less than a week."

"Would you rather live in a duplex in Sun City or a tent in paradise? Maybe he could build you a treehouse. Imagine making love in a leafy bower. It gives me shivers thinking of the possibilities."

"Those are farfetched fantasies, Kim."

"What if he decides to take the CEO position? If he stays, then go to work for the competition. That'll keep him on his toes."

"What was in that shot they gave you?" Jane asked dryly. "A hallucinogenic?"

For the entire ride, Kim wouldn't stop talking about Luke. She kept asking questions that made Jane squirm.

"Has he kissed you yet?" she pried.

Jane felt her cheeks burn.

"Ooh, ooh. Say no more. Your face tells the story. It was a lot more than kissing, wasn't it? You guys did the deed!"

"*Shh.*" Jane inclined her head toward the Uber driver.

Kim's mirthful eyes rounded wide. "What's Luke like in bed?"

"Hush," Jane said, almost wishing Kim had fractured her jaw instead of her leg.

"We've arrived at your destination, ladies," the Uber driver announced. "And for what it's worth, I think you should take your sister's advice. This relationship sounds like one worth exploring."

"Thanks for weighing in," Jane said, not feeling grateful at all, and helped Kim out of the van.

Inside their homey little duplex, Jane settled Kim on their well-worn couch covered by a red, white, and yellow-flowered chintz slipcover they'd made together. She changed sheets on both beds, washed some dishes, and cleared away debris that might trip her sister as she swung through the house on crutches.

"There's soup and snacks in the pantry and frozen dinners in the freezer. Use my account to order whatever other food deliveries you need. I'll also leave some cash on the table just in case. I'll drop your prescription off at the pharmacy on our way out of town, and you can have Melinda pick it up when she comes over."

"Thanks, but I'll be fine. You're the one who's starving." Kim's voice sounded slurred from the painkiller.

"Don't say it," Jane warned.

"Starving for love, that is. Really, Jane, Luke is a winner. All that thick hair, bulging muscles, and coppery skin. You'd never get cold at night cuddled up with him. Give him a chance."

"This is Arizona. I only get cold when you set the air conditioning too low."

"However, this turns out, I'm glad you hooked up with Luke and ended your born-again-virgin streak. Keep up the good work."

"Stop giving me a sales pitch about Luke Black. He's made it clear his lifestyle isn't compatible with long-term relationships. All I want from him is a tiny bit of cooperation—so I can get my promotion."

Jane checked her watch, wishing she had her own car. Why had she let Luke rush to the rescue? Jane didn't need or want a big strong man to solve her problems. When he arrived, forty-seven minutes later, Kim was so loopy from painkillers that she started telling him embarrassing stories about Jane.

Luke settled onto the couch next to Kim and egged on the stories. "So, she was a cheerleader in high school, huh? That's surprising."

"Why does that surprise you?" Jane asked, feeling a little defensive.

"Cheerleading seems fun, and you're not exactly a barrel of monkeys." He grinned.

"Oh," Kim said. "She was a lot more fun before our parents were killed. Get her to tell you about the time we snuck out to toilet paper the—"

"Luke," Jane said sharply, "we really have to get back. People are arriving at the ranch this afternoon to meet you."

"Sorry," he apologized to Kim. "When your sister's right, she's right. Can't have a circus without the ringleader."

Kim giggled. She seemed to think everything Luke said was hilarious.

"Take care now," he said warmly. "If you need anything, just give us a call. We can be here in two shakes of a lion's tail. Make that a monkey's tail. Papa lion is the laziest creature on earth. He does nothing but eat, sleep, and—"

"Luke, we have to leave!" Jane interrupted.

"Keep the lady lions happy."

"Should I call you Daddy Lion?" Kim joked.

"When will Melinda be here?" Jane asked, standing by the door, still reluctant to leave her sister alone but wanting out of this conversation.

"She gets off work at five." Kim's eyelids drooped.

"Meanwhile, you get some rest." Luke patted Kim's shoulder.

"Feel better soon." Jane blew her sister a kiss.

Kim pretended to catch the invisible kiss. "Right back atcha, lioness."

Ignoring that last bit, Jane latched on to Luke's arm. "I know you're procrastinating, but we have work to do."

"Bye-bye." Kim waved.

"Bye." Jane tugged Luke out the door, but she couldn't entirely shake off her anxiety. She supposed she never would when it came to her baby sister.

Chapter Twelve

BEFORE THEY REACHED the open convertible, a gust of wind blew sand across the yard. The eddies snatched up several loose pages of the confidential corporate reports that Luke must have left lying on the passenger seat, strewing them over the front lawn.

"Oh no!" Jane exclaimed, rushing to pick up the shattered documents.

Luke rushed to help.

"We're littering with sensitive company secrets. Your grandfather will—"

"Shh." Luke placed his hands on her shoulders as she clutched the recovered pages to her chest. "It'll be okay."

Then he lowered his head and kissed her thoroughly.

For a second, she sank into his kiss and allowed it to soothe her, but then she came to herself and pulled back. "Don't do that!"

"Relax, Janie. We'll round them up. It's not the end of the world." He rubbed the pad of his thumb against the frown line forming between her eyes.

"But if we don't find the missing papers, how can you know what's inside—"

"I've already read them all. There's nothing in them that interests me. I apologize for littering, and we'll pick up what we can find, but there are no corporate secrets in them. They're just corporate blah-blah, and I'm sure Ms. Polk could resend the documents online."

"I don't want to tell her we lost them."

He leaned over the Ferrari, picked up the remaining pile of papers, jogged over to the side of the building where the dumpster was partially concealed by a brick wall, and dropped them inside.

"Luke!" She chased after him. "You can't do that—"

"Already done."

She went on tiptoes to peer over the dumpster. The papers had landed on top of a pile of old food. It stunk.

Gak. She didn't want to crawl in there to retrieve them.

"Let it go, Janie." He strolled to the Ferrari.

Not knowing what else to do, Jane followed. "I don't appreciate you doing that."

"Understood."

"You're not going to apologize?"

"Nope." He hopped into the convertible without opening the door, *Dukes of Hazzard* style. Not something a dignified CEO should do.

Jane gnashed her teeth.

"Get in, Janie. We've got a date with bean counters."

Begrudgingly, she got in and buckled up. "Please, don't drive so fast this time."

"Your wish is my command," he said.

The freeway out of town was clogged with rush-hour traffic. Still, Luke always found an opening, leading the pack without being an exhibitionist or endangering anyone.

The revolution of the wheels hummed through her, vibrating from the soles of her feet. She wanted to put her hand on Luke's thigh and feel the surge of the engine pulsing through him.

Wanted to but didn't.

She was hot and thirsty. Closing her eyes, she imagined sparkling water, an azure pool with a classical nude statue, face raised to the spray. A nude that looked just like Luke.

Something nudged her arm.

"Sorry to bother your meditation, Janie, but the engine is overheating. Probably happened when we were stuck in traffic back there. I need to get water for the radiator."

"Oh, I didn't know." She was glad for the late afternoon sun, so Luke couldn't tell she was blushing from her fantasies about him.

"This is as far as we go until it cools," he said, sounding pretty cheerful for a guy whose car was acting up on a desert highway. "Good luck to us, though. If the GPS is right, we're only a half a mile from a gas station."

She looked around. "Uh-oh."

"What's that?"

"We're in Jackrabbit Acres. That's not a good place, Luke. The area is known for motorcycle gang activity."

"We're fresh out of options."

"We could call Triple-A."

"It would be faster to walk."

"August in the desert is no place to break down," she mumbled.

"It'll be okay. I'm with you."

That soothed her more than she cared to admit. Luke took her hand and guided her on the inside of the shoulder, away from the cars whizzing by.

People didn't perspire in the Arizona desert; they dehydrated. Jane's mouth was cottony, and her lips felt rough from dryness. Before they'd walked five minutes, she felt light-headed and slightly disoriented, as though this was part of some weird, surreal dream.

"Are you all right, Janie?" Luke stopped walking and touched her cheek with his knuckles.

"Fine, but I miss my air conditioning," she said, then giggled for no reason.

"Here's just the thing." He pulled a large red bandanna from the back pocket of his jeans and folded it to make a covering for her head. "Hang on. We'll get some fluid into you pronto."

Jackrabbit Acres had modernized the gas pumps, but nothing else. The combination saloon, general store, and all-around hangout was a long wooden building bleached silver by fifty years or more of blowing sand. A porch with dusty board railings ran the length of the place. A weathered wooden bench offered some blessed shade, but a trio of bikers had pretty much taken it over, sprawled out and guzzling beer while cussing the heat, their warm brews, and each other.

One of the men with shaggy, greasy blond hair and a filthy black sweatband seemed to be the leader. All three wore creased black leather pants and high riding boots. One wore a denim jacket with skull emblems on it. The other two wore leather vests over bare upper torsos covered by crude tattoos and sweaty, matted hair. They looked like they'd all spent time in prison.

Unnerved, Jane tugged on Luke's hand, hoping he'd skirt around them and follow a battered sign that said Deliveries in the Rear. Instead, he charged right up to the ugliest and biggest of the trio.

"A hog just like that one passed me five minutes ago," Luke said, pointing at one of the motorcycles parked a few yards away. "Great machine. I was doing ninety, and the rider had me eating his dust."

The ferret-faced biker was leering at Jane with bleary, red-rimmed eyes. She was too light-headed to do anything but cower at Luke's side and wish the earth would swallow her up.

Luke talked the talk, extolling the virtues of Harleys. Even Mr. Rodent-Face stopped ogling her and expressed an opinion about camshafts and pipes.

"It would a good race if you could catch up to the guy," Luke suggested. "I don't know how you'd do it, though. Same machine, five-minute head start."

The dirty-blond-haired man swore and spat, and the three bikers tossed their cans aside, mounted their bikes, and took off in a storm of dust and exhaust.

"Do you think they'll catch him?" Jane asked.

"Not likely." Luke grinned at her.

"You made that up?"

"Yep. It was too hot to take on all three," Luke drawled lazily. "So, I settled for a distraction. Sit here where I can keep watch on you from inside the store, and I'll go get something to cool us off."

"Okay." Jane wasn't thrilled about going inside with him anyway.

She leaned her head back against the splintery board wall, closed her eyes, and wondered where she'd get the energy to walk back to the car. Luke could pick her up here, but she didn't want to deal with any bikers on her own. *She* didn't know the lingo.

Luke returned shortly. "The owner's filling a gallon jug of water for the car. This bottled water isn't cold, but we can cool down another way."

She took a water bottle from him and looked skeptically at the battered pie tin he was carrying. "What do you have in there?"

"Ice cubes. The owner parted with them for a price. Lean back and close your eyes."

"Why?" She took a big swallow of warm water and then did as he instructed, closing her eyes against the arid heat.

"Let yourself relax," he said softly. "Trust me."

Yeah, Jane wasn't big on trust, but she wanted to get cool, so she tried to comply. He was only trying to help.

He lifted her right hand, cupped it in his palm, and then slid a cube over her sensitive inner wrist. After the initial icy shock, her skin numbed and absorbed the incredible, cooling dampness.

"It really works," she said with drowsy amazement.

"Shhh."

He slid another cube over her inner elbow, making her shiver with pleasure, then did the same to her other wrist and arm.

"Mmm."

The cubes were slippery now, and he ran one over her forehead and cheeks, then down to the V-shaped neckline of her lemon-yellow cotton knit top.

"I'm cool now, really cool," she gasped, guessing what he had in mind next.

The cube slid down to the hollow between her breasts, small and slippery but still cold enough to make her shiver.

"Enough," she begged, but he was already sliding a fresh ice cube over the back of her knee.

She had too much imagination. She couldn't help wondering how an icy trail up her thigh and over her bare hip would feel, Luke's cold fingers creating magic on overheated flesh.

"Oh!" Her moan came from way down deep and embarrassed her enough to break the spell. "I'm as cool now as I care to be."

She gulped more water to cover her agitation.

"I'm not."

"You expect me to—"

"Turnabout is fair play."

"But it's your game."

"You're cool and comfortable now. Fair is fair."

"Oh, all right."

He pushed the pan of rapidly melting ice cubes in her direction, stretching out his legs and resting his head against the wall.

She picked up a slippery cube and lifted his hand. His fingers curled when she stroked his wrist with the ice fragment, and she knew why he groaned with satisfaction.

Jane glanced over her shoulder, relieved there were no other customers, and fished another cube from the water forming in the bottom of the pan. She was enjoying this more than she wanted to admit. The contrast between the ice and the heat of his forehead gave her odd little shivers.

"There," she said when she finished sliding a piece over his throat. "You must be cooler now."

"Not quite," he whispered in a husky, spine-tingling voice. "There's still a lot of me to cool down."

His jeans had a single button above the suspiciously bulging zipper as a noisy pickup truck pulled off the highway, heading down the bumpy gravel road to Jackrabbit Acres. She scooped up the slippery remains of the cubes in one palm, quickly undid the button that held the waistband taut against his torso, and pushed wet ice pieces under the zipper.

He jumped up, slivers of ice falling to the ground from the leg of his jeans.

She was too embarrassed to look at him. Her mischievous trick had backfired badly. She'd accidentally grazed his junk with her fingertips, and now she'd come undone.

Mortified, she turned and started speed walking back to the car without him, castigating herself for sticking her hand down his pants in the first place. When he caught up, he was carrying a plastic gallon milk jug of water, and she was sitting in the car, trying to get control of her breathing.

He filled the engine with water, closed the hood, and got behind the wheel. Grinning, he drawled, "I owe you for that ice down the pants. So be ready, darling. I'll strike when you least expect it."

LEANING BACK IN THE seat with her eyes closed and her hair fanning out over the headrest, Jane feigned sleep, which suited him just fine.

He'd put the top up to protect them from more sun exposure and turned on the air conditioning full blast.

Luke was still amused—and thankful—for her prank. The ice down his pants had brought him to his senses, but she didn't need to know that.

Far from cooling him down, her touch had had the opposite effect. He'd wanted to follow the trickles of melted ice on her skin with his tongue. He'd ached to retrieve the slivers of ice between her breasts. He'd even been tempted to find out if Jackrabbit Acres had motel rooms to rent by the hour.

Fortunately, the cascade of wet ice down his legs had brought him to his senses. They'd had one glorious night together. A night they'd agreed not to talk about or repeat. And that was enough. No more sex. If they did, they ran the risk of getting attached, and neither one of them wanted that.

Or so he told himself.

But his mind started spinning *what-if* fantasies. What if Jane left her job and came with him to Africa? Life in the bush wasn't easy, and she was accustomed to the ease of first-world problems.

My world is not for you, Janie, he thought. He felt an odd tightening in his midsection when he glanced over and saw her long, spiky lashes flicker and the moist pink tip of her tongue touch her upper lip.

"Psst, Janie, are you awake?" He couldn't resist disturbing her any longer. He enjoyed talking to her almost as much as he'd liked planting a hard kiss on those softly parted lips.

She opened one eye. "What do you want?"

"Will our delay screw up our timing with the suits?"

"We should get to the ranch with a half hour to spare. That'll give us just enough time to shower and get ready for the meeting," Jane said. "Unless we run into trouble again."

Luke spotted that trouble as soon as he pulled into the driveway in front of his grandfather's ranch mansion. Two Cadillacs, a Mercedes, and a limo with a uniformed driver shining the windows. The company's big guns had arrived early, probably another of Rupert's ploys to wear him down.

"Oh, dear," Jane said with genuine distress.

He gave her hand a reassuring pat, then swung himself out of the Ferarri and went over to open the door for her. His philosophy on taking his licks was to get them over with.

"Why don't you go around to the kitchen door?" he suggested. "No need for both of us to get a dressing down."

"No, you were nice enough to drive me to Phoenix. It's my fault we weren't here when they arrived."

Arguing with her was like punching a wall of foam rubber: no pain and no gain. At least his grandfather wouldn't be here to give her a hard time. He did wonder who was high-level enough to rate the limo.

Luke led the way into the house, still wishing Jane would excuse herself. He heard the tinkle of ice in glasses and the monotonous buzz of business conversation before he saw the group standing around in the main room.

Three men in dark suits and conservative neckties were trying to kill time, probably saying the same old things they always said to each other. Then he saw the fourth visitor, his silver-haired grandfather, sitting in a big leather armchair like a king holding court. Hard to believe he had a heart condition.

"Luke, where the devil have you been?" Rupert grunted. "Homing said you had to chase down to Phoenix. Some kind of accident?"

"That's my fault, Mr. Cox," Jane said, gamely stepping forward. "My sister fell rock climbing, and Luke offered to drive me to the hospital."

"We net two million a year on gear for rock climbing. We could do a lot more business if—"

"Her sister will be all right," Luke interrupted, annoyed by his grandfather's obsession with business. "Thanks for asking."

"Glad to hear it," Rupert said automatically, clearly missing Luke's sarcasm. "But the two of you look like roadkill. Where are all the new clothes that I instructed Ms. Grant to buy you, Luke?"

The execs had inched their way to a far corner, out of their boss' sight but still able to soak up every word for later analysis.

"Did you study all those documents that I had Ms. Polk send?" Rex asked.

"Yes, sir. I'll be glad to sit down and discuss my thoughts on them after I've had a shower."

Rupert looked at his Rolex with more dials than a 747 cockpit and snorted. "Forget the shower. I'd like to hear your opinion right now."

Chapter Thirteen

FORGOTTEN BY THE MEN revolving around Rupert Cox, Jane slowly backed away, trying to blend into the shadows.

Luke plopped his dusty, sweaty, but still very sexy body into a white leather chair next to Rupert's spot.

She knew Luke had read at least some of the documents, but if her pupil flunked Mr. Cox's impromptu exam, she'd be the one at fault. She had failed to corral Luke.

Rupert steepled his fingers. "What do you think of the new products proposals? I thought the Serengeti-themed clothing line would be right up your alley."

"Do you want my honest opinion?"

"Absolutely." Rupert leaned toward Luke with aggressive body language that would intimidate most.

Jane cringed. In her experience, the last thing Rupert wanted on his company was honest feedback. Mr. Cox picked yes-men as his underlings. Except for Ms. Polk, no one ever made suggestions that didn't toe the corporate line.

"Adding new products would be a mistake. In fact, I suggest dropping your least profitable lines and maximizing promotional efforts where they can do the company the greatest good. For instance, in brand awareness and social media advertising. Instead of spending money on new lines, I say hire a media psychologist to help you get inside the minds of your consumers."

Everyone stared at Luke, including Jane. His suggestion made absolute sense.

"As I see it," Luke went on, "the 'bigger-is-better acquisitions of the last bull market left you strapped for cash flow and top-notch talent, so you made your management structure top-heavy. A common pitfall."

The minions in question closed in, sensing a threat to their domains—shaking their heads and mumbling disagreement.

Luke ignored them and went on with his assessment, making intelligent comments, pinning down problems like a corporate raider. For a man who didn't want anything to do with his grandfather's sporting goods empire, he was spouting facts and figures like an Ivy League MBA.

"How would you cut down on top-heavy management?" his grandfather asked shrewdly. "Attrition?"

"Too slow. Suppose you wait for the forty- and fifty-somethings to retire early. In that case, you won't have any vigorous young execs trained to breathe life into the company in ten years."

"So only young people can have inspiring ideas?"

"Not at all. But fat cats resting on their laurels rarely innovate."

Rupert seemed to consider this.

While his grandfather pondered, Luke kept talking.

Jane couldn't take her eyes off him. She was grateful he was performing so well but quite surprised by his astute comments. Was he softening toward his grandfather's request for him to take over as CEO? She found that hard to believe. He'd never be happy cooped up in an office dealing with petty office politics, not to mention wearing business suits and starched collars. His mind was too mercurial. His body always in motion. He was a cowboy at heart and always would be.

Why Rupert thought he should turn him into a corporate executive was beyond her.

As the conversation turned to the nitty-gritty details she didn't fully understand, Jane retreated to her room, grateful for a chance to shower. She changed into a sleeveless black crepe dress that, while simple, was dressy enough for dinner with the boss.

Or did she dare skip the meal?

She was only a lowly assistant to Mr. Cox's assistant, but unfortunately, the boss wanted her there. She dawdled in her room, dreading the time when she had to go downstairs. What was Luke up to? Sighing, she thought of inventing a headache as an excuse to miss the meal but didn't want to lie.

A nervous shiver tickled her spine as she walked into the room where the men were gathered. She halted, confused. Something was wrong.

Luke and his grandfather were standing near the front door. Rupert had his hand on the doorknob as Luke spoke.

Mr. Cox wasn't staying for dinner?

Rex raised his head and spied her in the dining room. "Ms. Grant, come here."

"Yes, sir." She scurried past the others to join Luke and Mr. Cox in the foyer. "What is it?"

"Didn't Ms. Polk give you the name of my barber in Sedona?"

"Yes, sir, she did."

"Then do your job. See that Luke gets there tomorrow."

Jane winced. "Yes, sir."

Turning to Luke, Rupert said, "See that you get your hair cut and your nails manicured before Saturday. There will be a little get-together at my country club. I want my friends to meet you. People you'll need to know. I'll expect you to accompany him as well, Ms. Grant."

"Yes, sir."

Luke didn't respond, but Jane could see the tension in his squared shoulders and clenched hands. His mouth was set in a tight line.

"Good night," Rupert said and walked out the front door.

Jane tried to convince herself that their relationship was none of her business. Still, she couldn't help wondering what motivated Luke to come to Arizona in the first place. Why was he staying when there didn't seem to be any warmth between him and his grandfather? What was keeping him here?

He muttered something that made her ears burn and gave her a frosty glance.

"Dinner should be ready," she said, falling back on an inane comment because she didn't know how to deal with the hurt in Luke's eyes.

"Enjoy," he said bitterly. "I'm not dressed for *polite* society." He stalked out the front door, too, leaving her to face the curious stares of the Cox executives.

"Will you be joining us, Ms. Grant?" asked the head of sales, Sal Mendenhall.

Was she supposed to play hostess? Obviously, these men thought so. They were practically standing in formation, waiting for her to give the signal for the meal to begin. She looked at the open doorway and made a rash decision.

"Please go ahead without me, gentlemen. I won't be joining you for dinner." She rushed out the door after Luke.

The Ferrari was still there. He must have decided to walk off his anger or frustration or disappointment—whatever it was that simmered between him and his grandfather—in the waning daylight.

Following the neatly manicured footpath that wound around the house, she hurried to check out the rear patio, hoping Luke hadn't taken to the road. She wouldn't get far in her heels, tracking him across the ranch.

She found him at the pool.

Checking for discarded clothing before she got too close, she saw the contents of his pocket and his watch on a small metal table beside a lounge chair. His shirt and jeans were crumpled on the plastic cushion.

Was he swimming in his underwear—or skinny-dipping?

She approached the pool with trepidation, standing on the edge until he completed a lap, broke the surface, and grabbed on to the rim a few inches from her feet.

"I'm sorry your grandfather didn't stay," she said.

"If you want to talk to me, come on in."

"I'm not in the habit of swimming in a dress," she said stiffly, trying to establish boundaries between them.

His hair clung to his head, showing off his terrific bone structure, those with high cheekbones and an aggressive jawline that went far beyond handsome.

"Live recklessly for a change if Rupert and his flunkies don't have you totally cowed," he challenged. "Take off your dress and dive in."

Why not? The evening was a bomb anyway.

She ambled over to the table, casually removed her watch and tiny gold earrings, then stepped out of her heels. With one quick zip, she let the dress fall to her ankles and stepped out of it.

Ignoring his low whistle, she stepped up to the edge of the pool in her ivory lace bra and panties and dived in. She did three fast laps before acknowledging him swimming alongside her, matching her stroke for stroke.

She paused at one end of the pool to catch her breath.

Luke swam up, trapping her between his arms when he slapped his palms on the lip of the pool. "Where did you learn to swim like this?"

"Not in a Montana swimming hole like you. My sister and I took lessons at the Y."

"You learned well."

He looked good wet—no, that was an understatement. He looked fantastic, droplets of water beading on sun-bronzed skin. His hair streamed water over powerful shoulders and trickled down the silky hairs plastered on his chest. His bared nipples made Jane uncomfortable, and she tried not to look at those hard, masculine points.

"You were angry because your grandfather left. Why?" She stared into his eyes.

"Let it be, Jane."

"If you're unhappy with him, why not just leave?"

"It's not that simple."

"Because of his health issues?"

"Among other things." He kicked away, swimming to the other end of the pool.

She didn't follow. She'd seen the way he looked down at her breasts, damply encased in almost transparent fabric, and was sure he'd come back to her. Was she in the pool to better understand him or to have him in her arms? She wasn't sure.

He broke through the water beside her. "I gave my word to stay in Sedona for thirty days. You know that, and I don't break my promises."

Well, she'd indeed been told off. The only reason to stay in the pool was to watch Luke slice through the water with heart-stopping ease and to avoid climbing out in her soaking wet underwear.

He did three more laps before he stopped beside her again. "Why aren't you swimming?"

"I can't thank you enough for driving me to the hospital," she said, changing the subject. "Kim really scared me when she called out of the blue. She's all I have, and family is essential to me."

"Not to me."

"Luke, you don't mean that. You came all this way to get to know your grandfather. Even with your differences, you still love him."

"I've satisfied my curiosity about Rupert Cox. That's all it was. Curiosity. Nothing else. Well, that's been sated. I'll go once my time's been served."

"I don't think that's true."

"Think whatever you like. I'm heading home at the end of August. Nothing can keep me here. I hope you understand,

Jane." He wasn't just talking about his grandfather. He was warning her not to expect anything from him, not to feel anything for him.

His warning came too late.

"Are you up to a race?" he asked. "My five laps to your three. Loser pays the penalty." His voice was light and teasing again.

"What penalty?"

"Winner's choice."

"I want you to get a haircut." She didn't, but she wasn't precisely in Rupert's good graces, so she pushed the agenda.

"Agreed, *if* you win."

"What do you want?" she asked.

"I'll think of something later." He gave a suggestive grin and wriggled his eyebrows.

"Luke!"

"If you're afraid you'll lose..."

"To you? I don't think so. On your mark, get set—"

"Go."

To his credit, he gave her a second's head start, then swept past her, hardly rippling the water. She wanted to win, needed to win, was counting on his extra laps to make it possible.

When he won by half a lap, she knew he'd been toying with her. He moved through the water like an Olympic champion, and a two-lap advantage wasn't enough.

"You knew you'd beat me." She was breathless and mad at herself for accepting a sucker bet.

"No, you're the one who made a contest of this."

She smacked the surface of the water with both hands, splashing spray in his face.

He only shook his head and laughed it off, drawing her into the circle of his arms and treading water.

"Do you want to know what your penalty is?"

"I can hardly wait," she said dryly.

"What I'd really like is to have you spend the night with me again."

"No!"

"Let me finish. That's what I want, but I agreed to back off on that, so I'll settle for a kiss."

"Oh, all right."

He reached down and cupped her skimpily clad bottom, drawing her so close his knee slid between her thighs.

Her entire body caught fire, and she had trouble catching her breath.

"You...you said just one kiss and nothing else."

"And I meant it."

Her stomach fluttered like a caged bird. Jane pursed her lips and closed her eyes, her pulse thumping madly. She wasn't stopping with one kiss. She wanted him again, and she didn't care if it was a stupid thing to lust after him or not.

She knew the deal. Luke was leaving. He hadn't left any room for negotiating, but that was okay. Hot sex was enough.

"A kiss at a time and place of my choosing," he said.

"This isn't it?" She felt weak with disappointment, or maybe the swimming competition had drained all her energy.

"No."

"So, you're not going to kiss me now?"

"Nope."

"I can't change your mind?" she asked hopefully.

He shook his head.

"Well, that sucks."

"You'll know when the time comes," he promised, pressing the tip of his finger against the end of her nose. "And I promise to give you fair warning."

"In case I want to back out?"

"Exactly."

"I don't want to back out."

"You say that now..."

"And mean it."

"We'll see." Then with that, he boosted himself out of the pool and strolled toward his clothes, one hundred perfectly buck naked.

Jane's jaw dropped as she watched him walk, his butt muscles flexing and releasing on his leisurely stroll. He didn't care who saw him. He was who he was, and he wasn't ashamed.

She wished she had ten percent of his self-confidence.

He stopped, paused, and turned to stare at her.

Feeling far more exposed than he was, Jane fell backward in the pool, submerging herself and allowing the gravity to take her down as the water closed over her head.

Chapter Fourteen

HAIR, HAIR, HAIR!

Jane wanted to scream. What was this obsession with cutting Luke's hair? He wasn't a

Marine recruit.

She rolled her eyes at the latest text from Ms. Polk. The woman insisted on a makeover for Luke before making his first official public appearance at Rupert's country club party.

If Rupert really was eager to have his grandson join the company, he should have enough sense not to make an issue over hair and nails. Luke wasn't a servile peon like everyone else—herself included.

He was who he was—genuine, authentic, one-of-a-kind.

Admittedly, barbers would starve if they waited for Luke's business. Still, Jane loved his shaggy look, the heavy sandy mane lightened by the sun and brushing his broad shoulders. It made him look unrestrained and untamed—and very, very sexy.

Especially in his cowboy hat.

She was starting to hate her job. Just being in the same room with Luke made her edgy. Maybe a good haircut would take away some of his sex appeal and make him look more ordinary. She hadn't urged him to humor his grandfather in the past several days, but the party was tomorrow. She had nothing to lose by suggesting it—if she could find him. He'd gone off by car or on foot every morning since his grandfather's visit, one time not even returning for dinner.

Respecting his process, she left him alone.

Whatever her boss expected her to accomplish here, she was getting paid for lounging by the pool. Anyone who thought she had a cushy job should try killing time as a vocation. It was considerably more challenging than actual work.

Loafing was, in a word, boring.

She was in luck today and caught up with Luke just as he headed out to the Ferrari.

"Are you in a hurry to go somewhere?" she asked, tagging along after him.

"Thought I'd go to the Grand Canyon and ride a mule to the bottom while I'm still in the area. Care to come along?"

"Done that, thanks. I started the trip feeling sorry for the mule and ended feeling sorry for me. The sun will broil your brains, and mobs of tourists will have the same idea. Spring and fall are better times of year to go."

"Afraid I won't be here then. But maybe..." Luke raked his gaze over her. "You have a better way to pass the time?"

Today he sounded more like the saucy cowboy she'd chased out of the fountain. The brooding, solitary Luke of the last few days was a little unsettling.

"I know a great little place in town—comfy chairs, soft music, personal attention...."

"Are you trying to con me into going to a spa, Janie?"

She shrugged her shoulders. "Thought it was worth a try. You're not going to cut your hair, are you?"

"Not unless you throw me over your shoulder and carry me there."

"Very funny. You're making my job awfully difficult, and Kim is counting on me getting that promotion to pay for next year's college tuition."

"I'm not falling for your manipulations," he said. "How is your little sis, by the way?"

"Doing pretty well." Jane paused. "Have a nice day."

"Wait a sec, Janie. My itinerary isn't written in concrete. Really, do you have a better idea of what to do with the day? And don't you dare start with that spa crap again."

"I'm not much of a tour guide, and Ms. Polk is riding my butt to get you that haircut and manicure."

He canted his head. "If you're persuasive, I might agree to a range cut."

"What do you mean?"

"A range cut is the way my cousins used to do it on the Montana ranch. I sit still for five minutes, and you click the shears around my head. Whatever comes off, comes off."

"*Me* trim *you*? Be serious! I can't cut hair."

"Sure, you can. There are tutorials all over the internet."

"Thank you for your confidence." She wasn't as put off by his suggestion as she wanted him to think. A range cut would be better than nothing considering Ms. Polk's adamant texts.

"Why not give it a shot?" he invited. "If you blow it, we can go with a buzz cut."

"Shear off that magnificent mane? No way."

"It's just hair, Jane. Give it go."

"Okay then." If Luke trusted her to get close to him with a sharp instrument, why not?

He went upstairs to shampoo while she watched a YouTube video. Once she thought she had the basics down, she borrowed scissors, a broom, dustpan, and a tablecloth to drape around his shoulders from Mrs. Homing. When he was seated on the patio overlooking the pool, she secured the cloth with a big safety pin.

"You and your sis have cut each other's hair, I imagine," he said, squirming a little while she made a center part with his comb.

"No way! Kim wouldn't let me touch her crowning glory for round-trip tickets to Hawaii," Jane teased, making a tiny tentative snip. "And I'm not about to let her play avant-garde artist with my hair."

"Ouch!"

"That didn't hurt," she said, wondering how to proceed. The YouTube video had seemed straightforward enough, but now, she wasn't so sure.

The stylist who cut Jane's hair parted it in sections and used clips to secure it. She tried dividing it that way with her fingers, enjoying the closeness to Luke. It made sense to start at the back and work around to the sides, but how much should she take off?

"A light trim," he said. "Just enough to show Rupert I got some taken off."

"Two inches?"

He shook his head, not doing anything for her concentration. "That's too much."

"At least one inch," she said firmly, doubting her employer would notice such a minor difference. But hair was part of a person's self-image; only the owner should decide how to wear it.

"It will take all day if you cut one piece at a time," he commented. "Or maybe you like being close to me?"

"No such thing!" she protested a little too vehemently.

She edged along, first one side and then the other. Luke's hair was nearly dry in the desert heat, warm and silky to the touch, but the ends crackled with life. The part she enjoyed most was checking for errant strands, letting his locks slip through the sensitive skin between her fingers.

Now all she had left to do was make sure the two sides were even. She stepped between his widely spread legs, combing to check for lopsidedness. His thighs felt hot against her bare legs, and she wished she'd vetoed his idea of doing this outside.

She was close enough to get dizzy on the faintly herbal scent of shampoo mingled sensuously with the musky smell of hot skin. Taking a side strand in either hand, she checked for evenness—and lowered the scissors when he suddenly clamped his thighs together, capturing her between them.

"You've cut enough," he said, gazing at her under lids hooded against the sun. "Tell you what. I'll tie it back for the party. Just for you."

"Thanks a lot." She laughed. "Let me go."

"I wonder..."

"What?"

"Whether you should pay your penalty now." He circled her waist and rested his hands at the small of her back.

"The statute of limitations on that has run out," she said.

"I don't think so." He was squeezing so insistently, she felt tipsy.

"I'm sure this state has laws against that sort of thing."

"Janie," he said. "You're so freaking beautiful. I'd pardon you if I were governor."

The dark shimmering in his eyes took Jane's breath away. She pursed her lips, waiting for the kiss.

It didn't come.

Instead, he stood, righting her to her feet along the way, never attempting to claim his kiss.

"The manicure is next," she said.

"Not happening."

"Luke..."

"Janie..." He grinned. "There is no way I'm sitting still while you paint my nails."

"Not painting. Just buffing and trimming and a hand massage."

"Now *that* sounds interesting."

Jane rolled her eyes, but at his comically raised eyebrows, her heart started beating faster.

He left with a hearty laugh, leaving her to sweep up hair and return the borrowed items. She tried to tell herself she was irritated because he didn't help to clean up. But she knew her disappointment went much deeper and closer to her heart.

TO JANE'S SURPRISE, Luke didn't give her any static about going to the party the next night. He met her in the living room, on time and resplendent in new pale-gray trousers and a tailored white shirt, the cotton so fine it was semitransparent.

True to his word, his hair was neatly tied back with a leather thong.

He looked, in a word, *gorgeous.*

"Very nice," he'd said in a low, sexy drawl, openly looking her over when she came downstairs in Kim's white halter dress. "Very nice indeed."

"It's my sister's dress," Jane said, sure she was blushing all the way to her toes. "I didn't even realize she'd put it in my bag until I got here and unpacked."

"Don't." He stepped close and brushed a tendril of dark hair from her cheek.

She suppressed a shiver. "Don't do what?"

"Don't be so self-deprecating. Don't give your sister all the credit. That dress is gorgeous because you're in it."

"Let's go," she said, knowing she should thank him for the compliment but unnerved by his observations.

She had absolutely no idea what to make of this man who did such strange and wondrous things to her equilibrium.

Smiling, he took her arm and guided her out into the warm desert night.

LUKE DROVE AT A SNAIL'S pace, by his standards, so he wouldn't miss the palatial home that served as a country club, hidden away in the hills on the outskirts of Sedona.

"Extra points for showing off," he said when they arrived at the ornate iron gate.

Jane giggled. "I agree. Look at the stained glass in the front windows. Who does that?"

"Apparently, my grandfather's ilk." Luke could think of much better places to take Janie in her stunning backless dress. The white set off her sleek, lightly tanned back and arms, and the short, flared skirt whirled tantalizingly above long, shapely legs. The dress made it hard to concentrate on anything else.

He could tell she was nervous about mingling with Rupert's snooty friends, and nothing he could say was likely to reassure her. He might do more harm than good if he said what he was thinking. That every woman there was sure to envy her. She had the kind of inner radiance few possessed.

"If we're not having fun, we'll leave," he said instead.

"We can't do that! Your grandfather—"

"We'll play it by ear."

Somehow, he'd get through this evening without confessing how he really felt about her. He'd thought of little else since the night they'd had sex, but he couldn't make one plus one equal two. Following a land management specialist into remote areas of Africa was no life for her. Taking over his grandfather's company was akin to a life sentence for him. They'd end up like his own parents had. Living apart and miserable.

He gave the valet the Ferrari keys, then put his hand under Jane's elbow and steeled himself for the dog and pony show.

"You must be Rupert's grandson," a blade-thin woman in a silvery, space suit sort of outfit said. She descended on them as they walked under a two-ton chandelier into the main room at the front. "I'm Amelia Wellington."

"Call me Luke. This is my friend, Jane Grant," he said.

"Ms. Grant, a pleasure," the woman said with the automatic charm of someone who'd extended the same welcome a thousand times. "The buffet is set up poolside. You can go out those doors and to your right. Later, I'd just love to hear all about your efforts in Africa, Luke. You're doing good work."

How did she know? Had Rupert been bragging?

Feeling caught off guard by the idea of his grandfather being proud of him, Luke guided Jane toward the pool with his hand at the small of her back.

People converged on them, pulling Luke one way and Jane another. She gave him an I'm-sorry smile as they were separated. He downed a glass of champagne and tolerated the small talk but kept searching for Jane in his peripheral vision. She was schmoozing one of the suits, laughing at something the man said.

Finally, Luke could escape his grandfather's entourage and tracked her down when she too was momentarily alone.

"Have you seen my grandfather?" he asked.

She shook her head. "I suppose he's fashionably late."

"Or he decided not to show up."

"I hope his heart isn't acting up."

That hadn't occurred to Luke. He'd been so ready to assume that Rupert had lured him to the party and then just stood him up. Now he was worried. "Me too."

"Maybe I should text Ms. Polk to ask about him."

"Just text him directly."

"Oh no." Jane shook her head. "I can't impose on him like that."

"Well, I can." Luke pulled his cell phone from his jacket pocket and texted his grandfather.

A text came right back. I've been detained. Enjoy the party.

Luke gritted his teeth. No real excuse. His grandfather had stood him up again. "He's not coming."

"The buffet is nice," Jane said, clearly trying to distract him. "Did you try the crab puffs?"

"Do you think I've been sufficiently introduced into polite society?"

"Luke, it's not even fully dark yet. Mr. Wellington went on and on about how terrific the grounds look when the lights come on. We should at least stay for that."

"This affair needs livening up," he murmured.

Jane hissed through clenched teeth. "Whatever you're thinking, please don't. You said we'd leave if the party wasn't fun. Let's just go."

"I have a new plan. Let's get the real party started."

"Luke." She cringed. "What are you up to?"

"Hide and watch, Janie. Hide and watch."

Chapter Fifteen

WARILY, JANE WATCHED Luke's every move.

He strolled over to one of the white-jacketed waiters replenishing the buffet and murmured something to him.

So far, nothing catastrophic, but she didn't trust him not to cause a ruckus.

After a lengthy conversation with the waiter, Luke went to the DJ playing staid music no one was dancing to. Then he stopped by one of the tables and lifted a bright red-and-yellow-striped umbrella out of the well in the center.

What in the world was he up to?

Luke separated the long pole, tossed aside the umbrella part, and recruited two dazed waiters to hold the ends.

Then turning to the crowd at large, he announced, "Limbo!"

The DJ launched into "The Limbo Song", playing it at a decibel destined to bring the police.

"The best sport takes the first turn," Luke announced, walking up to a woman with improbably thick hair piled high on her head.

"I haven't done the limbo since I was a Girl Scout." She giggled, looking for support from her bald, slightly paunchy husband, who gave an encouraging nod. Standing up, she put out her hand for Luke to take and followed him over to the pole like one of the Pied Piper's admirers.

"Show 'em how it's done, Maggie," someone called out.

She threw her head back theatrically and wiggled hips encased in a midthigh red satin skirt and went under the pole with a spate of laughter.

The game was on.

Jane watched with terrified fascination. Next, their hostess gyrated her hips and wriggled under the pole, followed by a plump, rusty-haired man who knocked into the bar and sent it flying.

After righting the pole, Luke took his turn, scooting his flexible body at the lowest rung so far.

The crowd gave a collective gasp and cheered.

"If there are more cowboys like him in Africa, I'm definitely going to Serengeti on my next trip," said a sexy blonde with an hourglass figure.

"One of the biggest thrills is a wildebeest ride," Luke said, strolling over to where Jane stood with the woman.

"I love exotic rides," the woman purred and lowered her lashes at him.

Jane wanted to kick her cosmetically enhanced rear end.

"I bet you do," Luke said to the woman, then turned to Jane. He went down on one knee in front of her. "Hop on board."

"Wh-what?"

"Hop on my back, and I'll give *you* an exotic ride," he said, his voice low and seductive.

Usually, Jane couldn't imagine complaining, but she'd had two glasses of champagne. She was feeling tipsy enough to override her own boundaries.

"C'mon, Janie." He cocked a grin at her. "Live a little."

"Do it," the blonde urged her. "Or I will."

That was all the catalyst Jane needed. Hiking up her skirt, she jumped onto Luke's back. Clamping her legs around his waist, the feel of his taut muscles against her bare skin drove Jane out of her mind. He was so warm and hard.

And she was getting wet.

Oh heavens. Someone hose her down.

He stood and trotted around the pool. Jane tugged the tie from his hair and ran her fingers through the lush locks, holding on to him like she was a princess and he was her pony. The limbo had turned into "Banana Boat" song.

Jane could hardly believe she was doing this. She was having the most fun she'd ever had. Since her parents had died and it was left to her to raise Kim, Jane had shouldered adult-sized responsibilities at far too young an age. Fun and frivolity had not been something she dared indulge.

When the music turned to the "Conga," Luke let her slide off his back and started rounding the guests up as he led the conga line.

Feeling breathless and amazed at Luke's stamina, Jane backed away from the action, suddenly all too aware of her role as Luke's keeper.

She failed on that score.

Big-time.

His head was thrown back as he shimmered and shook his body, leading the uproarious dance.

Unchained, the man was glorious!

And a rip-roaring success.

Everyone wanted to be near him.

Now chagrinned, Jane just wanted to crawl under a rock. There was no way she could ever keep up with a potent larger-than-life man like Luke.

As if sensing her withdrawal, he dropped away from the revelers. He came over, taking her hand and trying to get her to catch hold of the last person in the line.

"I'd really rather go home." She meant her real home, but for tonight she'd settle for the ranch.

"Janie—"

"Please stop calling me Janie," she begged. It felt too familiar, and she liked it too much.

"Ms. Jane Grant, the party is just warming up," he said. "Please stay."

"If you won't leave, then give me the valet claim ticket."

"Have you ever driven a Ferrari?"

She hadn't, and she couldn't imagine facing Mr. Cox if she got the slightest dent on a car like that.

"Never mind. I'll call an Uber."

"I'm leaving now," a dark-haired man in a tuxedo said. "Be glad to drop you off anywhere you want to go."

"She's with me," Luke told the man.

"Sorry." The guy held up both palms and backed away.

Just then her cell phone rang, and she dug in her clutch purse for it, peered at the screen, and groaned. It was Rupert Cox.

Wincing, she excused herself and went into the house so she could talk over the blaring music.

It was on the fourth ring and about to go to voicemail when she answered past the frog in her throat. "Mr. Cox, hello."

"Ms. Grant, excuse my language, but what in the hell is going on at my country club?" Rupert barked.

"Sir, I can explain."

"Please do. Some important people were there to look over my grandson. There are three board members in attendance, and believe me, they called me right away about his wild antics. It's going to be damn near impossible to get him approved as the next CEO, and it's all your fault."

"Excuse me?"

"It was your job to contain him."

"Mr. Cox, I am not a lion tamer. Luke is who he is. He's a grown adult. If anyone is to blame," Jane said, unable to contain her anger, "it's you. Time and time again, you've stood him up and let him down."

"What did you just say to me?"

"I'm sorry, sir," she said. "But you've got to know just how much your absence in his life hurts Luke."

"Because you're an exemplary employee," he said, "I am going to put your insolence down to alcohol."

"I'm not drunk."

"I'm offering you a chance to save your position, Ms. Grant. One last opportunity to civilize my grandson. Keep him under control, or you're out of a job."

"I don't want this damn job!" Jane exclaimed.

But it was too late. Rupert had already hung up.

"JANE?" LUKE CAME IN through the back door, feeling poorly that he hadn't agreed to take her back to the ranch when she'd asked. "Are you okay?"

Her hands trembled visibly, and her jaw was clenched hard enough to pop out the veins at her temple. Luke had never seen her so angry. "Your grandfather called me. He's got spies here at the party, and they're reporting back to him everything we've done." She shook her head. "I should have known."

"Did he fire you?" Luke asked, knotting his hands into fists. "Because of my behavior?"

"He didn't fire me...yet. He's giving me a second chance to tame you."

"You don't need him, Jane. You're a top-notch employee who could easily get a new job. If you want to quit, I'll support you until you can find a new position."

"No," she said. "I can't let you do that."

"How can I help?" He studied her face, feeling miserable that he'd backed her into a corner.

"There is something..." She waved her hand. "No, never mind. I can't ask you to do that."

"Do what?" he prodded.

She winced.

"What? Just name it, and I'll do it for you."

Jane sighed. "Maybe if you apologized..."

"Apologize! To whom? For what? All I did was liven up a deadly dull affair. I'd rather hang out with a bunch of hyenas waiting for leftovers than apologize for being me."

"It's just to smooth things over. It doesn't have to mean you're really remorseful."

"That's really what it's all about, isn't it? I'm just a pawn in Rupert's power ploys." He knew the truth. Knew his grandfather was using his poor health to manipulate him...using Jane.

Sweet Jane.

Caught in the middle of a family civil war.

None of this was her fault. She didn't deserve to be used as a puppet for his grandfather. Or as a receptacle for Luke's grievances.

"I'm genuinely sorry," he said, "that you got mixed up in this. And I am sorry that my behavior got you into trouble with my grandfather. But I can't apologize to him. I can't become a corporate yes-man for him. My grandfather is toxic."

"I understand."

"We're at an impasse."

"We are."

"What are you going to do?"

"I don't know. What are you doing to do?"

"Same thing." He shrugged. "I do know one thing, though; it's time to get out of here."

She held out her hand, and Luke took it, guiding her to the valet stand and then into the Ferrari.

With a roar of the engine, they tore off into the desert night.

By the time they reached the ranch, Jane was yawning, and any ideas Luke might have had about taking her to bed disappeared. She was exhausted, and her job was on the line because of him. Now was not the right time to seduce her.

Instead, he gave her a quick kiss on the lips and disappeared quickly before he had second thoughts.

JANE HAD STAYED AT Rupert Cox's ranch home for only two weeks, but it felt like two years. And her reason for being there was absurd—clean up his grandson's act. Much to her regret, she'd never met anyone less in need of transforming than Luke, and she'd been hell-bent on changing him.

Far from being the kind of untamed cowboy that his grandfather had made him out to be, Luke was considerate, self-confident, intelligent, and complex, fun-loving, and kind. Worse, he was devastatingly attractive—tall, strong, sexy, and charismatic. Jane thought about him constantly, recognizing that she was falling in love.

He was the perfect man for her except for one small fact. He'd be going back to Africa as soon as possible.

Would she go with him if he asked?

The way she felt now, she'd gladly live in a jungle treehouse to be with him, but she knew herself too well to pretend they could live happily ever after. She'd miss Kim like crazy, and, worse, she'd feel guilty for breaking up their little family. How could she leave Arizona and the only life she'd ever known for a man she barely knew? A man who had given no indication that he felt the same way about her.

Last night at the party, he'd gone too far. Without meaning to, he'd made her look ineffectual, at least in the eyes of Rupert's spy. But Luke was a full-grown, strong-minded man. How could anyone expect her coaching to make him executive material? She was trapped.

Even if she hated her job—and she was beginning to—she wanted to leave it with the good recommendations she deserved.

Bright and early the morning after the party, she got a call from Ms. Polk instead of the usual text.

"Really, Jane, Mr. Cox isn't at all happy with your performance. I think I should come up there and take over."

"No, I can handle the situation. Luke was just disappointed that his grandfather wasn't there, and he wanted to cut loose a little. Most people had a great time."

"I am curious as well why Mr. Cox isn't spending more time with his grandson, but that's none of our affair, Jane."

"I'll have a talk with him. See if I can get Luke to make the first overtures to mending fences with this grandfather," Jane said.

But hadn't she tried that last night? She'd asked him to apologize to Rupert, and he'd said no. What else could she do?

"Call me if you need me," Ms. Polk said. "I value you as my assistant, and I don't want to lose you. I am in your corner."

"Thanks," Jane said, feeling marginally better as she hung up.

LUKE TURNED AS JANE came into the dining room, his empty breakfast plate in his hand. He'd been staring at the serving dishes for over a minute, not seeing the food because his mind was replaying last night's incidents.

"Good morning," she mumbled and headed straight for the coffee maker.

"Hey." He wanted to add something more but didn't know what he could say to make things better. He'd gotten her into trouble last night, and he regretted it.

"Want to eat poolside?"

She shook her head. "Just coffee for me."

He set down his plate. He wasn't hungry either.

"You can eat, though. Mrs. Homing made all this great food."

"The suits are here," he said. "Some of them anyway. Mrs. Homing told me they returned last night while we were at the party. She put them up in the bunkhouse."

"Yes," Jane said. "There are those meetings you never got to. If you decide to stay."

That was a really big if.

"You're pretty down this morning," Luke said. "Can I do anything to cheer you up?"

She offered him a tight smile and plunked down at a table. "I'll be all right."

Luke sat across from her and sipped his coffee. Neither one of them spoke for a long moment.

Finally, Jane broke the uncomfortable silence. "What's keeping you here? Why aren't you on the way to the airport right now?"

"I gave my word," he mumbled, regretting his rash promise to learn to be CEO.

"You might have given your word to stay, but your heart has never been in it. You're here, but you're not trying. You've hamstrung me every time I've tried to help you."

What could he say? It was true. Jane was one hundred percent right. He'd acted like a rebellious teenager, and he wasn't proud of himself.

"You really want to know why I hung around?" he asked, ready to lay it all out there for her.

"Yes, yes, I do."

"At first, I stayed because I wanted to get to know my grandfather, especially when he revealed he needed a heart transplant." He paused, studying her stunning face. "But when it became clear almost from the beginning that he had no real interest in getting to know me, I stayed because of..."

"Yes?" Her voice went up slightly, and she leaned forward.

"You. I stayed because of you, Jane. You are the only reason I'm still here."

"ME?" JANE SQUEAKED, her heart pounding in her ears.

"You hadn't guessed?" He reached across the table to take her hand.

Her breath caught in her lungs at the pressure of his palm against her knuckles. "I thought...after the night we shared, I thought I'd blown it by leaving before you woke up."

"No, no," he said. "I thought *I'd* blown it."

"Really?" she asked, hardly daring to hope.

"Janie, I think you're incredible."

"I think you're pretty special too." She locked gazes with him, feeling her heart flip over.

"I wanted to talk about it but was afraid you didn't. I worried that I was complicating your life."

"You were," she said. "But in a good way."

"I didn't want to put more pressure on you...and yet I did. I feel bad about that."

"You're forgiven," she said lightly.

"Jane, I—"

"Mr. Black, hello," Mr. Cox's head of sales came into the dining room, followed by three lackeys. He was dressed in a suit and carried a briefcase. "Is this a good time to start our meeting?"

Without waiting for an answer, the man started unpacking his briefcase on the table between them.

"Look, Mr...."

"Mendenthal," the man reminded him. "Sal."

"Look, Sal, I'm in the middle of something here—"

"It's okay," Jane said. "Prove to me you're serious. Take care of business. When you're done, come find me. I'll be out by the pool."

Then with her crazy heart spinning dizzily in her chest, Jane walked away with her head held high.

Chapter Sixteen

AFTER SPENDING ALL day talking sales and marketing, Luke wanted nothing more than some quiet time alone with Jane. Luke had decided to focus and do all the things his grandfather had asked of him. For eight hours, thoughts of Jane had kept him listening to the corporate men drone on. It had taken every ounce of concentration he could muster, but he'd done it.

Now, he was ready for his reward.

Sweet Jane.

She was worth the misery of sitting still for one miserable hour after another.

He found her where she'd promised she'd be—poolside in the grotto, sipping a tropical drink and reading a book. She looked so gorgeous in the shadows; he had to stop and just stare at her.

"Mrs. Homing is serving a taco bar tonight," she said, glancing up to catch his gaze. "Are you hungry?"

He raked his gaze over her. "Oh, yeah."

Blushing, she got up, and they went to the dining room to load up on tacos. Rupert's men were there filling up their plates and still talking business.

"Back to the patio?" Luke asked Jane.

"Absolutely."

They snuck back to the grotto and ate soft tacos stuffed with beans, cheese, and shredded beef. They didn't talk much, just enjoyed the sight of mesas and each other's company.

It was calm. It was peaceful. It was bliss.

"What do you want to do after this?" Luke asked after a dessert of sopapillas laced with honey.

Her gaze latched on to his and held. "What do you want to do?"

"We could go for a walk," he suggested, not really wanting to do that.

"Take the Ferrari out for a moonlight spin."

"Hit up a nightclub in town and boogie until we drop," he offered in case she wanted to go out among other people.

"Or explore the game room. Maybe a round of billiards?"

"You're on the right track with fun and games," he said, lowering his voice. "But I imagined something more..."

"Physical?" she asked, a big old smirk lighting up her face.

"Yeah." He grinned. "That."

She stood up. "Let's carry these dishes inside."

"Yes, ma'am." He hopped up, bussed the table, and followed the sweet sway of her hips inside the house.

Clacking noises and murmured conversation came from the game room. From the sound of it, Rupert's executives had commandeered the pool table.

After leaving their dishes with Mrs. Homing, Jane took Luke's hand and led him upstairs. His heart was pounding so hard, he could barely think. Since they'd first slept together, Luke couldn't stop thinking about making love to her again, even as he'd told himself she was off-limits.

Now, Jane was the one taking control. Letting him know she wanted him as much as he wanted her.

On the landing at the top of the stairs, Jane turned to him. "My room or yours?"

"You're in charge tonight," he said. "Lead on."

Grinning, she ducked her head and escorted him to her bedroom. It smelled nice, just like her—floral and fruity.

Gently, Jane shut the door behind them, and they were alone. She wore the yellow bikini beneath a gauzy cover, and his eyes gobbled her up.

He hit the light switch with his elbow, desperate to see more of her. Jane's face, softened by passion, looked even more beautiful than usual.

She was trying to see all of him without seeming to stare, a becoming modesty he found endearing. He saw happiness and anticipation on her face, along with a touch of awe that flattered him immensely.

Her lids were delicate flower petals with downcast eyes, and her slightly parted lips were temptation incarnate. Luke prayed she wanted him at least a fraction as much as he wanted her. God, she was the most beautiful thing he'd ever seen.

"Luke," she whispered, her voice thick with passion.

Yes, the reward for doing his grandfather's bidding was worth it, but he couldn't keep taking a back seat. His hands twitched to touch her.

"Janie," he whispered right back. "Sweet, sweet Jane."

Practical, common-sense Jane disappeared as she wantonly reached for the buttons of his crisp white business shirt. He'd worn the button-down to the meetings to prove he was all in with Rupert's plan to turn Luke into a mini-me clone.

Her fingers at his buttons were like an electric current running through his body. Everywhere she touched, he tingled.

Luke was edgy. He'd been dreaming of this moment ever since they'd made love the first time. Trying on one fantasy after another. Jane and him going out in the pool. Jane on the table in the grotto, on the park bench in the desert. Jane in a tent on a red rock mesa. He'd been tormenting himself. Keeping his hands off but feeding his daydreams.

This was so much better than his wild imaginings. Soft and welcoming. Leisurely paced and long-lasting.

He felt like a volcano about to erupt, but he wanted the night to be as memorable for her as it was sure to be for him. For tonight was more than a casual hookup. No quick fling. Luke was fully invested, and he knew Jane was too.

Where is this going to lead? whispered the doubting voice at the back of his mind. The voice that reminded him often that he was a handful and not built for polite society. He knew his brain worked differently from most; he had accepted that a long time ago. The hard part was, how did he and Jane fit? If he stayed in her world, he'd need a total personality overhaul, and he wasn't sure how to accomplish that.

Shut up, he told the voice—something he was skilled at. Shutting down the naysayer inside him was how he survived. He followed his gut, not his head, and right now, his belly was urging him to merge with Jane at all costs.

Somehow, with fumbling on his part and nervous giggling on hers, they managed to strip off each other's clothes, tossing clothes around the room like discarded tissues.

Naked, he fished condoms from his trousers and set them on the bedside table. He turned down the covers and, with a flourish of his arm, bowed to Jane. "After you, my love."

Love? Had he really said that?

Cringing, Luke froze, worried he'd made a huge goof, and he'd chase her off.

But Jane came over, wrapped her arms around his waist, and beamed up at him. *Whew. Okay.*

He cradled her to his chest, and she flicked out that wicked little tongue of hers, tickling the hollow of his throat. Then she slid down his body, wiggling lower to catch his nipple between her teeth, teasing it. At the same time, her fingertips drew lazy circles on his stomach, moving a little bit lower each time.

All the things he'd dreamed of doing during long, restless nights alone were possible now, but the joy of being with her overwhelmed him. It didn't matter what they did together. It was what they meant to each other that counted.

He gently stroked her breasts, so enchanted by the velvety smoothness and the pebbly flesh surrounding her erect nipples. All his urgency and apprehension were transformed into intensely pleasurable arousal.

She was on her knees now, her mouth so near where he ached for her to go.

"We have all night," he whispered in her ear. "If you keep doing what you're doing, I won't last a second."

She leaned back and looked up at him, stretching languidly. For one instant, a temptress revealing her full breasts, then a bashful lover linking her fingers to conceal her nakedness.

"Come here." He moved to the edge of the bed and patted the mattress beside him, his voice sounding oddly muted in his own ears. "Please, Janie," he begged without shame.

She snuggled beside him, looping her left leg across his right and her hand resting between them.

His arsenal of sensual tricks had always seemed more than adequate, but how could he possibly please this woman as much as she deserved? He wanted her to melt with longing and climax repeatedly until she experienced all that he had to give her.

"Aren't you going to kiss me?" she asked shyly.

"Oh, yeah." He kissed her softly at first, then heatedly, filling her mouth with his tongue until her breath was as ragged as his. Turning, he straddled her hips and lavished kisses on her shoulders, her breasts, and the length of her torso, nuzzling her, his tongue finding her sweetest spot.

After a long moment of kissing, he tenderly removed his mouth from hers. "Are you absolutely sure about this?"

"Do you really have to ask?"

"I don't want you to have regrets in the morning."

"The only regret I have is that you're stalling, cowboy. How come?"

"Things are complicated for us."

"Not right now," she said. "You can turn off the corporate image tonight. It's just me and you here, Luke. Feel free to be yourself with me."

That was what he'd been looking for—her permission to be himself.

"I just wanted to make sure you're going into this with your eyes wide open," he murmured.

She purposely widened her eyes and her grin and pulled him down on top of her. "Hush up talking, cowboy, and do what you do best—act."

Freed by her permission to be himself, Luke did just that.

Thirty minutes later as Jane stroked him with her magical fingers and gasped, "Now!" Luke went all in.

He flipped her onto her back and sank as deeply into her soft, willing body as he could go.

Trembling with urgency, he held back for as long as he could, wanting them to come as one, loving her with his whole being, joining his body to hers.

"Oh, Luke! Oh, Luke!"

"Yes, Janie, yes. Just let go. I've got you. Turn loose."

The orgasm scream that ripped from her throat joined his own guttural sound. Luke clutched her to his chest. For the first time in a very long time, he no longer felt so alone.

JANE AWOKE SLOWLY IN the first light of dawn, remembering she'd fallen asleep still linked to Luke. His hand was heavy on her breast. And even though nights were always cool in the desert, his flesh against hers was overheated in the bedroom.

But minor discomforts were overshadowed by total awareness of the man cradled against her. She reached across his hip and lovingly patted his round, firm backside. Then she tickled the slight hollow at the end of his spine until he groaned with pleasure and threw his leg across hers, locking her even closer against him.

He awoke slowly, too, kissing her in all the little places he'd overlooked the night before. Then he parted her thighs and caressed her with the tip of his finger until she squirmed with pleasure and invited him to say good morning in the nicest possible way.

"That," she said sometime later, "was even better than last night."

"Each time with you gets better and better," he said.

They lazed in each other's embrace, tenderly trailing fingers over sensitive spots, laughing, teasing, talking about nothing and everything.

"I'd love to stay in bed with you all day," she said. "But you've got another full day of meetings."

"Don't remind me," he groaned, putting a pillow over his head. "Yesterday just about killed me. Sitting still just isn't my jam."

"There's one thing I don't understand," Jane said. "If you wanted to connect with your grandfather, why are you so reluctant to do the things he's asked of you?"

"I tried, Jane. I really tried to do what he wants. He doesn't get me. He doesn't understand that I'm not the kind of guy who just can't sit behind a desk and shuffle papers. It would be a death sentence to me. I know that sounds dramatic, but I've never been able to sit still, not even when I was a kid. Especially when I was a kid. It's one of the reasons my mom left. I was too much for her. She couldn't handle my rambunctiousness."

"Oh, Luke." She interlaced their hands and rubbed her thumb against his. "I am so sorry your mother couldn't love you for who you were." She paused. "Or Rupert either."

"It's okay," he said. "I had my dad and his side of the family. I have my cousins, and we're closer than brothers. And in my job in Africa, no one expects me to be anything that I'm not. I guess I got used to the freedom of truly being me. It's hard to fit yourself in someone else's box."

"So why are you even trying?"

"Rupert reached out, and he was sick and looking for family. I'm all he's got."

"Hmm."

"Hmm? What's on your mind, Janie?"

"It seems to me like you have two choices."

"And what's that?"

"Let go of trying to build a relationship with your grandfather. Go back to your life knowing you have done the best you could to connect to very different people. Or you can accept your grandfather's conditional love and do what you came here to do. Prove to him you can be what he wants you to be."

"Both of those options are painful."

"Which I suppose is why you're still here."

"No, Jane. It's not. I'm here because of you."

"You barely know me, Luke."

"I know you far better than you think I do." He rolled over onto his side, brushed a lock of hair from her forehead, and peered deeply into her eyes.

Her breath caught at the depth of feeling she saw in his eyes.

"I know you can't get going without a big cup of black coffee in the morning. I know you try hard to do your very best. I know you're a loving sister and a great employee. I know you worry too much and that your heart is just a little too big for this world. I see you, Jane. And I think it's been a very long time since anyone has really seen you for the competent, magnificent woman that you are."

His words stirred her in the feelings that swelled in her were very close to love. Not just for this man, but for herself. The self she'd put aside to raise her sister after her parents had died. The self that did its best to make a difference in the world. She was a good person. She did mean well.

"I see you, Janie. Fully."

She wanted to believe that so much. Wanted to build on their powerful sexual attraction. However, something still gnawed at her, something she hadn't been able to put her finger on until now—something that had flummoxed her about Luke.

Jane thought of all the ways Luke's behavior had confused her. His inability to be idle. His craving for action and adventure. His poor time management skills. His impulsiveness. His problem focusing on dull tasks. His dislike of reading.

Gasping, she sat straight up in bed.

"What is it?" Luke stared at her. "What's wrong?"

"Has anyone ever told you that you might have ADHD?"

"No." But he looked interested, canting his head, studying her intently. "What makes you say that?"

One by one, she listed off the behaviors she'd observed in him, behaviors that sometimes led to his detriment. Starting the limbo at the wrong party. Pushing the sports car too hard in broiling hot weather. Bully confronting a biker gang on his own.

"Your mother said you were a handful, right?"

"Yeah."

"Maybe that was just because you had untreated ADHD."

He shrugged. "Could be."

"Can you imagine how much easier your life might have been if you'd had the right help?"

"I dunno," he said. "I think I turned out pretty decent."

"Oh, you did. But if you'd been giving a road map for how to navigate the world full of people whose brains didn't work like yours, wouldn't that have been helpful?"

"I guess so. I always thought of those traits as part of my personality, not something wrong."

"What if what you see as your personality was actually a dysregulation in your brain?" she asked, almost sure now that Luke had ADHD.

He looked at her for a long moment, saying nothing, his eyes hooded and thoughtful. "What are you suggesting?"

"I'm saying," she said in an excited rush. "There's a way to fix you. A way you'll be able to connect with your grandfather and do the things that you need to earn your place as the next CEO of Cox Corp!"

Chapter Seventeen

LUKE DIDN'T HEAR A word that Sal Mendenthal was saying.

The head of sales for Cox Corp stood at the front of the conference room, using a laser pointer to call attention to something on a PowerPoint presentation projected on the screen. His mouth was moving. But the words that came out of it sounded like the *wonk-wonk-wonk* of adults in the *Peanuts* cartoons.

All Luke heard was his own brain repeating what Jane had said when she sent him downstairs for the meeting.

I'm saying there's a way to fix you.

As if he was broken. As if he didn't fit in.

That shouldn't come as a shock. Over the years, many people had called him names. Handful. Wiggle Worm. Jumping Bean. Crazy Legs. It had hurt then.

And it hurt now.

Despite all that talk about letting Luke be who he was, she didn't mean it. She thought he was broken.

Maybe she was right. Maybe they were all right. Luke was the odd duck. The one who didn't fit. Not everyone else.

The message she'd given was loud and clear even if she hadn't come right out and said it. *If you want to be me with Luke Black, you better figure out a way to fit in.*

Inhaling deeply, Luke forced himself to pay attention to Sal. Just when he was getting the gist of what the man was saying, a knock sounded at the door.

"Come in," Sal invited.

The door open and Jane poked her head in. "Sal," she said. "I'm afraid we'll have to cancel Luke's meetings for today. Something important has come up."

"Anything I need to know about?" Sal asked.

"No," she said. "I just need for Luke to come with me."

He was glad to get out of the meeting, but somehow, Luke felt uneasy about this reprieve.

AFTER DROPPING RUPERT Cox's name to the receptionist of a top-notch neurologist in Phoenix, Jane arranged to get Luke in to see a doctor that very day.

On the drive to Phoenix, Luke was unusually quiet.

The fact that he could have a mental processing disorder must be overwhelming. Jane didn't prod him to talk, and after a round of tests at the doctor's office, they received the diagnosis the following day.

Jane's intuitive guess had been right.

Luke did indeed have attention deficit hyperactivity disorder.

The neurologist recommended medication, and at Jane's encouragement, Luke agreed to give it a try. She picked up the prescription that afternoon while Luke sat through more meetings. She was so excited for him. Thrilled that he would now have a way to fit in with his grandfather's world.

"This is going to change everything for you," she reassured him the following day when he downed the first pill. "You'll finally be able to do everything your grandfather has asked of you."

"Yay," he said, but his tone was gloomy.

"Luke? Do not want to take the medication?"

"No, no, I want to be able to pay attention like everyone else. It would be nice to be normal." He smiled, but it seemed forced.

"It's okay to feel conflicted. It'll be a big change." She remembered what the doctor had told Luke and how the things that confused him before would make sense to them once the medication kicked in.

"I'm sure it'll take some getting used to." He kissed her. "Now show me how to tie a Balthus knot, so I can run circles around Sal Mendenthal and his half Windsor."

He dressed in the conservative blue pinstripe suit that she'd put out for him, and she watched the process with a smile on her face. Looking at her handsome man never got old.

Her man.

When had she turned so possessive of him?

"You're gonna knock this thing out of the park, Luke. Your grandfather is going to be so proud of you." She paused and kissed him on his chin. "And so will I."

"What are you gonna do all day while I'm pouring over spreadsheets?" he asked, glancing longingly at his blue jeans, Stetson, and cowboy boots sitting on a chair in the corner.

"Don't you worry about that. I've got a terrific evening planned to reward you for a hard day at the office."

"Trying to outdo yourself, Janie?"

"You'll have to wait and see." She winked and sent him out the door, with a kiss and a promise for the night that lay ahead.

FOR THE REMAINDER OF August, their days passed in a pleasant sameness.

Luke noticed an immediate change in his ability to concentrate on the medication. He had to admit that while he wasn't crazy about how the drugs reduced his spontaneity, they sure helped him fit in and toe his grandfather's corporate line.

The managers and department heads finally left the ranch, and the Homings took a week vacation. In the end, he and Jane had free run of the ranch. By day, she taught him etiquette and social graces. By night, he taught her how to fully enjoy herself in bed. Or in the pool, or on the hood of the Ferrari, or on the billiards table.

They took trips into Sedona, where he cheerfully went to the spa with her and sat still for a manicure and what his grandfather called a "proper" haircut. Jane actually shed a tear watching his locks fall to the salon floor. He teased her for her attachment to his hair, but he missed it too. But now, he fit in. The sacrifice was worth it, he told himself. To gain his grandfather's approval, a polished persona was required.

They hiked the red rocks and visited the vortexes. They took that Jeep tour, and it was as fun as he'd imagined, and for a couple of hours, rumbling on the mesas and through creek beds and streams, he felt like his old, wild self.

He could do this. Play a role to suit society and then find an outlet for himself on the side. The medication did help with that goal.

Nights were the very best time when he and Jane dropped their inhibitions and fully explored each other. The time passed in a blur of sensuous pleasure. They indulged in role-playing games and teasing and tempting each other. They watched soft-core naught flicks, and Jane read to him from erotic poems.

They gave each other foot massages, and Luke taught her a thing or two about toe sucking that blew both their minds. They luxuriated in the hot tub, having fun with those throbbing jets. They took food to bed and licked chocolate syrup and whipped cream off each other's bodies. They fed each other strawberries and let the sweet, sticky juices drip over their hands and mouths.

Unfortunately, the fun had to end.

The month was over. His grandfather was throwing a Labor Day party to officially welcome Luke to the company.

There was only one step left. Luke had to decide if he was going to stay in Arizona or go back to Africa.

And Jane held the key to his decision. Luke was rapidly falling in love with her, and before he could commit to his grandfather's company, he had to know if what he and Jane had was really real.

He wouldn't ask her for a commitment. Their relationship was still too new for that. But at the Labor Day party, he planned to tell her how he felt.

From there, the rest was up to her.

THEIR LAST NIGHT ON the ranch was special. They cooked steaks on the grill and shared a bottle of wine from Rupert's wine cellar. They talked and talked and talked. He told her about his life in Africa. She told him about her struggles bringing up Kim. They discovered they had more in common than they initially thought. They both loved country music and southwestern art. They'd watched the same TV shows as kids, and they'd both taken short-lived violin lessons. They had both grown up with lots of pets—dogs and cats and rabbits for Jane, cattle and horses and dogs for Luke. They both adored Rocky Road ice cream, and neither of them cared for soda. The more they talked, the more they learned about each other and the closer they got.

The night was so special and passed so quickly. It was midnight before they knew it. The Homings would be back the following day.

Then Luke, with just a little wild man left in him, stripped naked and jumped into the pool. Laughing, Jane shucked off her clothes and followed.

The night air was cool, but the pool water was warm.

"C'mere," he called to her.

She swam to him.

His lips were cool from his swim as they closed over hers, kissing her so deeply she had to cling to his shoulders for support. She felt the grainy texture of his tongue and the ivory smoothness of his teeth as his lips moved, making the long, hard kiss an act of love.

The man wanted her.

Her body was electrified; her nerves were on fire. She forgot how she came to be in his embrace and returned his kisses with all her heart and soul. When he scooped her into his arms, it was a homecoming, the place where she longed to be forever.

"I love this ranch," she whispered. "I wish we could live here forever."

"We could make it a real ranch, not just some corporate hideaway."

He was speaking as if planning for their future. It was a heady notion. Jane enjoyed hearing it, but she was skittish too. It wasn't right to make plans with her if he didn't intend on staying in Arizona. She knew the issue wasn't settled. He and Rupert had never bonded the way Luke had hoped. She wasn't going to let herself get caught up in what-ifs. All that mattered tonight was she and Luke in each other's arms.

Later, they could sort out the rest.

She was falling in love with him. She couldn't help herself on that note. But being in love with him didn't mean they were right for each other. Only time would tell on that score.

When he climbed from the pool and put his hand out to boost her, she took it. She let him pull her up beside him and then gently dry her off with a fluffy pool towel.

Then they made love on the circular patio daybed, and it was better than every other time before.

THE NEXT MORNING, THEY left simultaneously, chasing each other through the hills of Sedona, Luke blasting past her in the Ferrari, then slowing down to let her catch up.

They arrived in Phoenix together but split off at Interstate 10. Luke going right toward Rupert's residence, Jane angling left, headed for home.

He honked his horn and waved at her as they separated. She smiled and waved back.

She'd ended the month tanned and relaxed and having learned how to have fun. She might have tamed Luke, but the wild cowboy had unraveled her uptight self, and she was in a hurry to go back to prim and proper Jane.

They wouldn't see each other until Rupert's Labor Day party at his mansion in the chichi part of Phoenix, on the opposite side of town from where Jane lived. She had insisted on the breather. The last two weeks had been so magical as to feel dreamlike and mystical. They needed to ground themselves in reality. They needed time apart. Jane needed to touch base with Kim, and Luke finally needed to have a heart-to-heart with his grandfather. She'd even gotten him to agree not to text her. It was less than a week until the party. If their feelings for each other were solid, it would withstand a little distance.

What she hadn't expected was how she couldn't shake him from her mind. He dominated her nights, too, popping up in her restless dreams. And by the time the Labor Day party rolled around, she was a total basket case.

The question was, were her feelings for him an obsession? Or was this true love?

She tried not to make herself crazy over it. Only time would tell whether their romance was nothing but a sweet dream or if it was something to build a solid life on.

JANE WAS SURPRISED at how nervous she was to see Luke again. Her heart was in her throat as she drove to the party, dressed in Kim's skimpy white halter dress, her hands tightly clutching the steering wheel.

Tonight, she would learn how successful she'd been in transforming Luke into the man his grandfather had always wanted him to be. Jane shifted uneasily. It was starting to fully dawn on her just how manipulative Rupert had been with his grandson, using Luke's desire to connect as something to dangle over Luke's head.

Dirty pool, she thought.

Also, tonight, she'd learn if she'd get her promotion. It had once meant so much to her, but suddenly, she wasn't sure she wanted it.

Not at Luke's expense.

She parked her car in her usual spot, passing the fountain as she went into the building. Her memory strayed to the day she'd seen Luke in the pool in all his wild man glory. Uninhibited. Free. Spontaneous.

Gosh, she loved that man!

Maybe tonight, if things went well, she'd tell him how she felt. Lay her cards on the table. Let the chips fall where they may.

She practiced on her walk to the door. "Luke, there's something I need to tell you."

No, that sounded ominous.

"Luke! I love you!"

Nope, that was too overwhelming.

"Luke, I've been miserable without you."

Nah, too clingy.

The security guard spied her and opened the door. “Welcome back, Ms. Grant.”

“Thank you, Gary. Has Mr. Black arrived yet?”

“Just got here. I wanna say, you did a bang-up job straightening that guy out.”

“Thank you,” she said, but it didn’t feel like something anyone should thank her for.

She approached a group of employees waiting for the elevator, and they were all buzzing about Luke. Jane paused, listening to their conversation.

"Oh my gosh, I can't believe he's the same man. When he first showed up here, I was certain Mr. Cox had lost his marbles. Wanting to put a cowboy in charge of the company," said a forty-something project manager in a red sheath dress.

"Me too. Wowza! I mean, he was hot before, don't get me wrong, but now he could make the cover of Forbes," said her friend who worked in the same department.

"I wonder how he'll change the company," mused a male employee named Zack, who worked in the marketing department. He stuffed his hands in his pockets and rocked forward on the balls of his feet.

“Jane is going to get that promotion you’ve been shooting for,” the woman in red told Zack. “How could she not?”

She shouldn’t be listening to this. Jane turned to go, but instead of leaving the area, she ducked behind a column to eavesdrop.

"Hey, no one offered to pimp me out as sex bait," Zack complained. "If that's what it takes to get a promotion, I'd do it."

"Luke doesn't play for your team, honey." The woman in red touched his arm.

"Do you think there's a way to sue the company over this?" Zack asked. "Sexual impropriety or something. Handing out promotions to employees who willing use their bodies to get promoted?"

"Jane would have to be the one to sue," said the woman in red. "And why do that if you don't have a grievance with the system?"

The elevator dinged, and the people got on. The doors slid shut, and Jane collapsed against the pillar, her heart aching as if she'd been stabbed straight through it.

What Zack has just said was absolutely true. From anyone else's point of view, Rupert Cox had used her as bait to tame his grandson and bring him into the fold.

Her sexuality had transformed Luke into a corporate stooge.

At the time, Jane hadn't seen things that way. But now? Well, now, there was no way she could continue to work here.

Chapter Eighteen

THE PENTHOUSE ROOF was packed with employees having a good time. There were games, and a live band and a photo booth, and far more food than the people gathered could possibly eat. Jane wondered how Luke felt about the overabundance of hamburgers, hotdogs, and barbecue from the viewpoint of someone working in food insecurity.

How could he possibly be okay with his grandfather's wasteful lifestyle? How could he adopt it as his own?

What had she done to him?

Misery crawled through her. She had to quit. Tonight. She had to tell Rupert Cox precisely what she thought of him.

Careful. You still need a good recommendation from Rupert.

She wasn't going job hunting with a big black mark on her record, not after selling her soul to the devil, so to speak.

Shame filled her.

Attempting to mold Luke into something he could never be had been wrong from the beginning, and she should have had the guts to stand up to her boss much sooner. Her judgment had been clouded by sexual attraction. She'd been willing to go along with anything to stay near Luke.

And that was the truth of it.

Her empty stomach painfully knotted, her mind buzzing with the things she wanted to say to her manipulative boss.

But she had to own her part in it as well. She'd let the promise of a promotion turn her head. She should have refused the assignment. She was complicit in Luke's undoing.

Jane searched the crowd for Luke but didn't see him. After hearing what she'd heard in the lobby, she didn't want to mingle, knowing what people were saying about her behind her back.

Just leave.

It sounded like sound advice. Tightening her grip on her clutch purse, she turned to head back down the elevator.

"Jane! There you are!" Rupert strolled up to her, beaming from ear to ear, Ms. Polk hovering behind him.

Ugh. She was trapped.

Not really. Tell her boss off and then get out of here.

But she couldn't do that. Not the way she wanted to do it. She needed to give two weeks' notice, and she needed a recommendation. Best to buck up, put a smile on her face, make some lame excuse about why she was quitting, and then exit.

Without talking to Luke?

None of this was his fault. He was the injured party, not her. She'd gone into this with her eyes wide open. Too bad she hadn't understood the ramifications. She'd been a fool.

"I'm about to announce both your promotion and Luke's new position with Cox Corp," Rupert boomed.

Luke's new position. Apparently, tonight was the night everyone learned Luke was going to be the CEO.

Fresh misery bit into her. Luke was accepting a position ill-suited to him, and it was because of her.

Rupert took her elbow. "Come along with me to the stage."

"Sir," she said, gathering her courage. "Before you do that, we need to have a talk."

He looked surprised. "Is something amiss, Jane?"

Just then, the elevator door opened and a freshly shaved, shorn, and polished Luke, resplendent in a conservative pinstripe suit and burgundy silk tie, stepped out. A tie knotted in a full Windsor.

She hadn't seen the total package of Luke imitating his grandfather's image of him. He was, in a word, a knockout.

Her jaw dropped, and her heart skipped, and she felt suddenly like bawling her head off.

Initially, he didn't see her, greeting employees as he moved into the party. She watched him a moment, longing for this man and hating herself for having a significant role in his metamorphosis. He was smiling and charming, articulate, and gracious, shaking hands with board members as if he'd been doing it his entire life.

Where had the spontaneous, fun-loving cowboy gone?

You medicated him.

Here was the question. Was Luke better or worse off because of it?

"Can we put that talk on hold for a moment, Jane?" Rupert asked. "I see someone I need to schmooze. Grab yourself a plate from the buffet, and then meet me in my office in thirty minutes."

"I-I..." She was about to tell him no, that they needed to have the discussion right now. Still, Rupert charged across the room to the lieutenant governor who'd just stepped off the elevator with his bodyguards.

Luke still hadn't seen her, which was just as well. She was still under his spell. The spell that had convinced her to do something that went against her moral code. How could her feelings for him be real when he was no longer the man she'd fallen in love with?

Feeling sick to her stomach, she placed a hand on her belly and drew in a deep breath of arid night air.

The memory of their sexy nights together was branded on her consciousness. The pain of knowing she'd lost sight of herself was almost too much to face. She refused to nurture even the slightest hope that they might have a future together.

Luke had gone full-on corporate.

And she was to blame.

She was sorry he'd cut his hair short enough to make him almost unrecognizable as the wild cowboy who showered in fountains.

Just go, just go.

But Rupert was standing between her and the elevator. And he was sure to see her if she went past.

She noticed people staring at her with sidelong glances and murmured whispers. Thanks to Zack and the project manager in the red sheath dress, she knew what they were saying. Jane Grant sold her body for a promotion.

"Congratulations, Jane."

She glanced over to see Ms. Polk smiling at her in a motherly way. "You outdid yourself with Luke. Mr. Cox and I are so impressed."

Maybe so, but she wasn't proud of herself.

Ms. Polk—her reserved, all-business boss—came closer and put her arm around Jane's shoulders. Jane's stock seemed to have skyrocketed as if she'd just been voted into an exclusive club, but it was one she didn't want to join.

She pulled away from the woman. She was about to tell her she was quitting, but she wanted to deliver the message to Rupert first. He'd told her to meet him in his office in thirty minutes. She'd just go there now.

"Jane?" Ms. Polk said. "Are you okay?"

"I need to excuse myself," she said, easing toward the elevator, poised for flight.

And nearly collided with Luke as she started to race-walk across the room. "Jane," he said, a big smile crossing his handsome face. "There you are."

She stared at him, hurting so badly she couldn't speak. Knowing now that everything had been a setup, a manipulation. She couldn't trust her feelings. Couldn't trust herself. She was naïve and gullible.

"Jane?" His eyes, dark blue and searching, examined her face with such intensity she was forced to look down at his black wingtips. So different from the scruffy cowboy boots he preferred.

She'd ruined him. That's all there was to it.

"What's wrong?" He reached out for her hand, but she shied away. A worried expression flared in his gaze.

She wouldn't answer, and she wouldn't even think about his hard round bottom. Or other spectacular attributes wearing in the chaste white underpants she'd ordered for him from Javiar.

"I have to leave."

"Wait, and I'll come with you."

"No!" The last thing she wanted was for him to talk her out of her resolve. To tell her she was silly for letting other people's opinions of her drive a wedge between them. It would be so easy to close her eyes and ignore reality. To tell herself because she hadn't intended on having sex with Luke that it had been okay to accept the challenge of civilizing him in exchange for a promotion.

She'd destroyed the man he'd been and all over her own gain.

The shame was unbearable.

She felt as though she was standing nearly naked in front of him again, only this time her emotions were being scrutinized, not her body.

"Are you really going to take over the company?" she asked as a smokescreen to avoid saying something she might later regret. She had to start thinking of Luke as just another mistake but forgetting him would be the hardest thing she'd ever done.

Rupert came up to them. "I'm ready for that talk now. Luke, could you entertain the lieutenant governor while I have a private conversation with Jane about her promotion?"

Luke stuffed his hands in his pockets, then seemed to realize that it was unpresidential and removed them. "I will."

Rupert took Jane's elbow and guided her toward his office on the back side of the bank of elevators. She wanted to jerk away from his grasp but was reluctant to cause a scene. There were enough eyeballs on her already.

"Mr. Cox," she said in a low tone. "There's really no need for a discussion. I need to resign from my position. The way you manipulated me into changing Luke's behavior is unconscionable, and I'm humiliated that I was party to it. Because of me, you've turned a wonderful, interesting man into your clone when all Luke ever wanted was to get close to you. I hope you'll do the right thing and give me a glowing reputation, but even if you don't, I can no longer stay at Cox Corp. I've lost all respect for you...and myself. Good day, Mr. Cox."

And then she did jerk her arm away from him, raced to the exit door, plunged into the stairwell, and raced down six flights of stairs in high heels.

LUKE STOOD IN A DAZE, watching Jane run away as he walked up to his grandfather after he'd turned the lieutenant governor over to Ms. Polk. He'd heard Jane tell Rupert she was resigning.

He felt as though he'd been hit in the midsection by a wrecking ball.

"What's gotten into her?" his grandfather asked rhetorically.

Which was good because Luke didn't have an answer for him.

The fire door to the stairwell was closed now. But the soft *tap-tap* of Jane's heels echoed in his head. He could hardly believe she'd not only walked away from her promotion, but she'd left her job.

Why?

He'd done everything she'd asked. Turned himself inside out for her, and she wouldn't even stay and talk things through with him.

Luke realized his grandfather was watching him with a shrewd expression. "What is it?"

"She's quite a gal," Rupert said.

"Yes, she is," Luke agreed, angered that his grandfather had managed to chase her away. "What in the hell did you do to her?'

"I have no idea."

Was Rupert really that clueless?

"You and I need to talk," Luke said grimly. "No more weaseling out of the hard conversations, Grandfather."

Chapter Nineteen

JANE DIDN'T GO RIGHT home after quitting her job. She didn't want to face Kim. Not until she could give her sister a logical explanation for why she'd thrown away her career, her promotion, and probably her bonus.

She didn't want the bonus anyway. It was tainted money. She especially didn't want to explain about Luke. The pain was so fresh and searing, she couldn't bear to tell her sister how she'd allowed herself to be used for crushing a good man. If she told Kim, she might bawl, and sympathy would be her undoing.

"Jane, grow up!" she told herself bitterly. Happy endings were for storybooks. She had to focus on survival. The rent would come due just as it always did. The landlord didn't care if she had a broken heart or not.

She drove around until it dawned on her she'd better save gas for getting to job interviews. Then she walked through Walmart, but there was nothing in the store to distract her, especially since even a new tube of lipstick was no longer in her budget. She had friends who found solace in retail therapy, but Jane was too practical for that kind of self-indulgence.

Finally, she went home, and for the next two days, applied online for any job remotely in her skill set. Kim was unusually sensitive, not asking her questions or offering advice.

As a stopgap, Jane signed up for temp work, and there was a chance she'd get called to work a few days the following week. Somehow, she and Kim would survive financially, but Jane knew her emotional recovery was a long way off. She'd fulfilled an impossible assignment, taming Luke, but it had cost her a job and her heart.

And it had cost Luke his dignity whether he knew it or not.

Two nights later, she worked on a resume, understanding that nothing she wrote would help her get a suitable permanent position. Not unless her former employer gave her a satisfactory reference. She dreaded talking to Ms. Polk and hadn't done anything about asking for a letter of recommendation or cleaning out her desk.

Just the thought of it left her feeling like a ragdoll.

Trying to cheer her up, her friends invited her to go to the movies to check out a new heartthrob collecting rave reviews for his acting chops. Jane went along, feeling a tad guilty about spending the money, but she had to do something to shake off the doldrums. The exciting new star was a pallid blonde too young to interest her. In fact, she was afraid no man would ever appeal to her after Luke on celluloid or in person. *Charisma* wasn't just a word to her anymore. She'd experienced it up close and personal. Got so swept up in Luke's sex appeal that she'd lost herself.

The instant Jane got home, she suspected something was up. Kim had a coy, all-knowing expression that suggested she was in the mood to play mind games.

Jane blew out her breath and braced herself.

"Did you have a nice time?"

"The movie wasn't bad," Jane said. What was Kim up to? "What have you been doing?"

"Studying. Being on crutches should be good for my grades."

"Nothing else?"

"You forgot your phone."

"Did I?" Good grief, she'd been so absentminded because of Luke she hadn't even noticed she'd misplaced her phone.

"Yep." Kim pointed at her phone lying on the coffee table.

Jane moved into the living room to pick it up. The thing probably needed charging.

"Oh, by the way, Luke texted. He really wants you to call him."

"You read my text messages?"

Kim shrugged. "You're the one who left your phone behind."

Jane didn't like the way her pulse started racing at the thought of a text from Luke. Since he hadn't tried to contact her the last few days, she'd assumed he'd decided to let things between them fade away, for which she'd been grateful. She didn't need closure with him. Their whole relationship had been orchestrated by Rupert and Ms. Polk. There's been nothing real about it.

Well, except for the orgasms.

"I don't think so," she muttered, more to herself than Kim. She didn't even pick up her phone to read the message he'd sent.

"Jane! You *have* to call him." Kim hopped on one foot over to Jane's cell phone on the coffee table and held it out to her.

"Wouldn't it be easier to use your crutches?" Jane asked in the big-sister-knows-best voice she knew irritated her sister, hoping to distract her from talk of Luke.

"Call him, Jane. He's really eager to talk to you. Please?"

Instead of taking her cell phone, Jane walked out of the room and left Kim holding it with a perplexed look on her face. She simply couldn't handle talking to him right now. If he tried to sweet-talk her into seeing him again, she wasn't sure she had the strength to stay away.

Unfortunately, she did have a few things to pick up at the company. Especially a picture of her mother and a cut-glass flower vase that had been her great-grandmother's, but she'd kept putting it off. Confronting Ms. Polk would be bad enough, but how could she be sure Luke wouldn't be there? She couldn't imagine anything more awkward than running into him at the office.

By Monday of the following week, she had two job interviews scheduled for Thursday and Friday, but the temp work hadn't materialized. She was still on the list, but they didn't need her yet.

She came home in the late afternoon after signing up for Workforce with paperwork to fill out and barely enough energy to toss them on the kitchen table.

Her cell phone buzzed, letting her know she had a message. Jane held her breath, telling herself she didn't want it to be from Luke again but desperate to have some connection with him. She felt like half a person, functioning on the outside but numb inside. Hating her weakness, she whipped her phone from her pocket.

The text wasn't from Luke. Disappointment swept through her.

Ms. Polk texted: Dear Jane. Please schedule a time at your earliest convenience to clean out your desk.

Jane paused, then texted back: Next Monday?

Ms. Polk: We'd prefer sooner rather than later. We've hired your replacement, and she starts Monday.

That was a kick in the gut. Jane had never worked anywhere else besides Cox Corp except for waitressing jobs when she was a teenager. It was official. She was out.

Ms. Polk: Could you drop by at nine tonight?

Jane: Why so late?

Nine sounded good. Luke was less likely to be there after hours. Maybe her old boss was giving her a graceful way out.

Ms. Polk: It's September inventory. I'll be working until midnight if you need to come later.

Might as well get it over with. Sighing, Jane texted back: I'll be there at nine.

Ms. Polk: I'll have the security guard look out for you.

THE WALKWAY FROM THE employees' parking lot to the administration building was well lit at night. The pinkish glow made it a bit eerie as Jane hurried toward her old workplace at exactly nine p.m. She didn't mind being on the spacious grounds after dark, knowing security guards were on duty. Still, the area around the fountain made her uneasy. She approached it with trepidation, remembering this was where her heartbreak had begun.

Shadows played across the illuminated display, the water cascading day and night upward to dazzle any passersby who otherwise might not be impressed by the Cox complex. She supposed it was an advertising statement, the same water endlessly recycled in a city that had blossomed in the desert.

Her eyes started playing tricks on her again. She caught a glimpse of movement, probably only the play of light on the spray. Still, it gave her pause. A vagrant could be on the grounds, and she didn't know how far away the closest security guard was.

Should she run to her car? She hadn't bothered to change out of her casual white shorts, tank top, and sandals, so she didn't have the disadvantage of heels and a skirt if someone chased her. Still, she was no sprinter, and her best bet if threatened was probably a good ear-splitting scream. Should she keep heading toward the office complex or retreat while she could?

She would love to forget the whole thing, but the guard in the main lobby was expecting her. It would be cowardly to abandon her possessions, especially a photograph that meant so much to her. She very much wanted to put everything about the Cox Corporation in her rearview mirror so she could get on with her life.

She'd brought a canvas bag to carry her things. She slipped her purse into it, giving the tote some weight in case she had to use it to defend herself. However, she didn't suppose it would do more than momentarily startle an attacker. Cautiously, she crept forward, her gaze riveted on the pool, ready to scream and flee if someone was hiding there. Much as she'd like to turn tail and run, she didn't want to be embarrassed by a second request to clear her desk.

There was movement.

Oh heavens, there was someone in the fountain.

Her pulse thundered, and she had a split second to make her decision: dash away to the parking lot, streak toward the building, or confront whoever was in the fountain.

That's when she realized it was Luke.

This time the man under the spray wasn't a naked cowboy. Instead, he was fully clothed, in dress slacks and a new white cotton shirt sticking wetly to his torso. He also had a tie—this time a bow knot—done up at his throat.

She hadn't even taught him the bow tie since it was pretty tricky, and she wasn't accomplished at it herself.

Her heart was pumping blood throughout her body so hard and fast, she felt heated from the inside out.

"What on earth are you doing in there with your good clothes on?" she asked, knowing full well she was getting sucked into his stunt.

"Keeping cool while I wait for you." He stood as still as a statue, water still raining down on him.

"I'm only here to clean out my desk," she said, quelling the desperate urge to run. If Luke started saying sweet things, she couldn't hold firm. "Ms. Polk is waiting for me."

"I doubt that," he said, walking out from under the spray but making no move to wring out his streaming hair or brush the water from his strong, handsome face. "Ms. Polk is on her honeymoon."

"Honeymoon? That can't be—I mean, she texted and told me to get over here. I never dreamed—who did she marry? When—"

"She and my grandfather had a simple civil ceremony this afternoon. They're on their way to Paris as we speak."

"Ms. Polk married to Rupert?" Her jaw dropped. "Why did Ms. Polk text me then?"

"It didn't look like you were going to call me back, so I persuaded Ms. Polk to arrange for you to come here."

"She had no right—"

"Don't blame Ms. Polk. I badly need to talk to you," he said in a quiet voice that sent shivers down her spine.

"I hope the guard will let me in. Now that I'm here, I really do need to pick up my things." She was trying to ignore the pathetic way he was standing in ankle-deep water, looking half-drowned in what had been nice clothes.

"You may not want to pack up your things just yet," he said.

"Of course, I do."

She kept telling her feet to move, but they seemed to have taken root on the pavement. "I meant it when I resigned."

"There may be a nice position for you at another location after the corporate restructuring," he said. And he took a few steps closer until he was on the verge of stepping out of the pool of water surrounding the fountain.

"What restructuring? With you as CEO, doing a job you hate? No, thank you."

"Come on in and cool off," he invited her with outstretched arms. "I'll tell you all about it."

"No way. You come out here if you want to talk. You're ruining your new pants." She instinctively backed away, mistrusting herself, not Luke, if he came too close.

"I won't be needing them." He stepped onto the rim of the pool, his bare feet making a little swishing noise.

"You...you're going back to Africa?" Her throat tightened with hope. Had he woken up and realized just how much his grandfather had used her to manipulate him into becoming something he wasn't?

Honestly, did it matter whether he took over his grandfather's job or hightailed it back to the bush? Either way, he was out of her life. She simply couldn't trust what they'd shared. Their romance had been as manufactured as *The Bachelor*.

"Janie," he murmured with yearning in his eyes. "Will you please listen to me? I know you're upset, and you have every right to be, but there's more to the story than what you know."

She hesitated like a fool.

He stepped down on the pavement and moved closer, letting her see that his rugged features were softened by desire. It was a look that didn't require words, but she didn't know what to make of it.

"I need you, Jane." He took her in his arms, and she didn't resist.

Sighing deeply before his lips brushed tenderly against hers, his kiss was so sweet and satisfying, Jane lost herself in it, wanting it to last forever.

She could feel the tickle of his breath on her cheek and hear the sensual murmur that welled up in his throat. The world around them ceased to exist as her senses filled with him. This was why she hadn't answered his text. She knew she'd be unable to resist him.

Helplessly, she dissolved as he stroked her back and teased her lips apart with the tip of his tongue.

She loved the taste of his mouth, the texture of him, the heady pleasure of being wanted. She loved him.

He buried his hands in her hair, holding her head while he nuzzled her nose and ear, his lips so gentle they tickled.

"No," she said, wrenching away from him. "I can't do this again."

He cupped her face in both palms, held her head still, forced her to look at him. "What is it, Jane? What did I do that was so wrong? I tried so hard to be who you wanted me to be. Where did I go wrong?"

Seeing his pain broke her heart all over again.

"That's exactly the problem, Luke. By trying to please me, you ceased being you."

Chapter Twenty

"I DON'T UNDERSTAND." Perplexed, Luke shook his head. He'd done everything she'd wanted, and that's why she'd ghosted him. It seemed illogical.

She peered at him, and her eyes were so mournful it took everything he had not to glance away. For the first time, it occurred to him his silly grand gesture in the fountain wasn't going to sway her.

It had startled him when she quit Cox Corp, but he'd decided it was the pressure of coming back to the real world after their idyllic time at the ranch, and he'd give her some space to sort through things and come to her senses.

Then when he'd texted her and she hadn't responded, his feelings had gotten hurt. He thought they'd had something special in Sedona, and he moped around for a few days, feeling sorry for himself.

After that, he'd taken matters into his own hands and, with Ms. Polk's help, lured her here tonight. He had to take one more stab at it. She was worth fighting for. If following this, she still wanted to walk away, then he'd have to accept it, but not before he made his pitch.

"Talk to me, Jane. If this is going to work, we have to be able to communicate."

"We can't work, Luke."

"Why not? Help me understand."

She clenched her jaw and looked as if she wanted to run away, but she took a deep breath and said, "When I saw you dressed up like Rupert's clone, it broke my heart. I destroyed you, Luke. I put you on medication. I calmed you down. I turned you into someone else entirely. You were no longer the man I fell in love with."

"You fell in love with me?" he asked her, feeling as if his heart was being ripped from his chest.

Silently, she nodded.

"Janie, I love you too."

"You do?" Hope flared in her eyes, and her hope stoked his.

"Yes, yes!"

"How can you love me when I basically sold my body to your grandfather for a promotion?"

"What?" Confused, he shook his head. "What are you talking about?"

"I didn't realize that's what I was doing," she babbled. "When your grandfather offered to give me the promotion, I'd been dreaming of a big bonus if I could teach you some manners. It seemed pretty straightforward and aboveboard. But then we had sex, and things got complicated, and I just let myself live in a fantasy. It was easy in Sedona when it was just the two of us but outside that little bubble..."

"What?" he urged, desperate to understand her thought processes.

"Seeing you meditated and dressed up and spouting spreadsheet data around Rupert rocked me to my core. And when I overheard the employees gossiping behind our backs,

I realized everyone thought I'd slept with you to get you to do what your grandfather wanted. And I was so ashamed. I couldn't face them, and I couldn't face you. Because that's exactly what I had done. Not intentionally, but that was the results."

"Oh, sweetheart, is that all?" Tears misted his eyes. He was that touched that her concern for him had fed her false sense of guilt. "Please don't worry about what other people think. All that matters is what we think."

"Well, Luke, I think I wronged you."

"No way."

She held her fingers to tick off her flaws. "I badgered you into getting a haircut. I—"

"Jane," he said sternly to snap her out of her anxiety. "I did those things because I wanted to."

"To please me!"

"No," he said. "I did it because you helped me realize how my inability to focus had narrowed my options in life. You were the one who recognized I had ADHD. All these years, I'd felt so different from everyone else, and I didn't know why."

"Really?"

"The medication didn't turn me into a corporate drone. It helped me concentrate. Suddenly, I understood why school had been so hard for me. What you gave me was a tremendous gift."

"I did?"

"Oh yes. My brain works the way it works. There's really nothing I can do about that. I'd managed to find workarounds that helped me function. I lived in societies—on the ranch in Montana and in the villages of Africa—where the way my mind worked was an asset and not a liability. But if I want to be the best that I can be, I need tools for when I'm in places or with people where my mind is a hindrance. Before, I was shooting blind, hit or miss. Now, I've got medication to use when I want to concentrate. And tricks and techniques to navigate different kinds of environments, and I'm not stuck with only a few career choices. I have options now that I didn't have before. Thanks to you. Janie, I owe you my new life."

COULD IT BE TRUE? HAD she honestly helped Luke instead of tying him down?

His hair was damp but drying quickly, as all things did in Arizona's arid climate. She ran her fingers through it, combing the shortened strands with her fingers.

"I'm sorry you cut your hair. I love it long."

"It will grow." His voice was husky with passion, and she was afraid to believe this was happening.

"So, you're going to take over as CEO of Cox Corp?"

"No."

He was going back to Africa. She'd known since the beginning, but that didn't make it any less painful. How could she go back to an ordinary life without him? "You're leaving Arizona."

"Yes."

Would he ask her to go with him? If he did, could she say yes and leave behind everything she'd ever known? Leave behind Kim and her friends?

"I have some things to take care of in Africa, but I'm coming back."

"To Phoenix?"

"Come sit by me." He perched on the edge of the fountain and patted the marble beside him.

"Tell me the coming back part first."

He got to his feet in one fluid movement and took both Jane's hands, standing in front of her with a boyish grin. "I knew when you quit your job, you were nuts—or crazy about me—to throw away your promotion when you'd more than earned it."

"Now you sound cocky."

He kissed her. Then kissed her again, the moon shining liquid gold around the shadows.

She pulled back. "You're avoiding my question, Mr. Black. If you're not going to live in Africa and not run Cox Corp, what will you be doing? And by the way, why did you turn down the job of CEO?"

"How could I be CEO without you on my team?" He tilted her chin and smiled down on her, his sapphire blue eyes easily the most beautiful she'd ever seen.

"You promised your grandfather that—"

"The trouble was," he said gravely, "I didn't like being blackmailed into staying. I wanted to get to know my only blood relative on my mom's side, but Rupert didn't seem to have any time for me. I was angry—mostly at myself for making that dumb promise to take over for him, and I'd never intended on staying...until I met you."

"You're still beating around the bush. Where is this going, Luke?"

He stroked her hair, combing it with his fingers. "I've never seen thick dark hair as fine as yours."

"Luke!" She couldn't get mad at a man who made her feel like a goddess, but he was driving her crazy, leaking out bits of information instead of telling her the whole story all at once—the tease.

"Sorry, Janie." He brushed a soft kiss on her lips and lovingly patted her backside. "I should tell you about my talk with Granddad."

"Please do."

He reached over to interlace their fingers. Holding hands with him felt so good.

"I had a long talk with Rupert after the Labor Day party." He paused again. The man was driving her bananas.

"What did you discuss?"

"I told him the changes I wanted to implement when I take over as CEO." He laughed softly. "I'm not one to run a sweatshop. I favor a relaxed workweek with flexible hours and on-site childcare. I also want to implement company-sponsored wilderness retreats for employees at the ranch in Sedona, plus add some productivity incentives like stock distributions."

"He'll never agree to *any* of that."

"No? You should have heard what he had to say about my ideas on building a more diverse and varied workforce. You've already heard what I think of all the deadwood in the upper echelon."

"What was his reaction?"

She was breathless in anticipation, wondering if Luke had toe marks on his backside from being booted out.

"He decided he's been a little hasty about his decision to retire. Even though he had a heart attack, it was mild, and he is only sixty-two." Luke chuckled. "He isn't so sure I'm CEO material when he does step down."

"I don't understand."

"We hashed things out bit by bit for several days. Went deep in a way I hadn't expected we would. Turns out he wanted his grandson in his life, and he thought the only way to guarantee it was to hand over the company. Of course, he planned to stick around to give advice."

"He was using the business to hide his feelings?"

"Yes. He had a lot of regret over my mother and didn't know how to express his grief. I behaved like an idiot keeping him at arm's length. Part of that was his conflict with my dad. Seems he was afraid I'd bolt if he came on too strong as the repentant granddad. My mother ran away because he was too heavy-handed and demanding. He didn't want that to happen with me, so he thought the best way was to tie me to him through company responsibilities."

"What about his sudden marriage to Ms. Polk?"

Luke covered her knee with his hand. "What do *you* think?"

"I know!" she said, stopping his hand on its upward trip, so he didn't distract her from getting the whole picture. "Your grandfather married his original candidate for CEO. If not his grandson, then his wife would be his logical replacement when the time comes."

"Ms. Polk been his mistress and right-hand assistant for years," Luke said sheepishly. "I should've tumbled to it when she went off on the haircut crusade. It was a wifely thing to do, not what an executive assistant would insist her boss' wayward grandson do."

"You two have wasted a lot of years," Jane said with a new compassion for grandson and grandfather. "What will you do now?"

"Now that I'm all 'civilized'?" He wriggled his eyebrows.

"That's doubtful, but I'm glad you're not at odds with your grandfather anymore. Even though he can be overbearing, I think he's just a lonely man who missed his family and used the company to fill the holes."

"Tell me, Janie," he said, taking her hand in his. "What would you think about a new position?"

"Like what?" she said, her pulse taking off at a gallop. She did love this man, but she wasn't sure she was ready for a marriage proposal this soon in their relationship.

"Ranch foreman."

"Ranch foreman?" She blinked. "I have no experience in that."

"Oh, I beg to differ. You sure can tame wild cowboys. I'm certain you'll be able to run a ranch just fine."

"What ranch?" she asked, scarcely daring to hope. "Who would I be working for?"

"Me." He burst into the biggest grin she'd ever seen. "I'll be running the ranch in Sedona. It'll be for team-building retreats. Granddad did like a couple of my ideas, and I'll be running it as a real ranch and going back to school to get my master's degree now that I have the tools to help me study. That's why I need a ranch manager I can trust. Then he named a figure double what she would have made with her promotion."

"Are you serious? That's absolutely perfect." She peered into his eyes. "For us both."

"Yee-haw!" he exclaimed.

"Once a cowboy, always a cowboy, I suppose."

"And don't you forget it."

He kissed her again. A long and hard and passionate kiss that made her tingle all the way to her toes. "I love you, Jane Grant. I love you immensely, immeasurably, unceasingly. Together, I think we make the perfect team."

"I can't believe this is happening!" Her happiness was bubbling up and almost overwhelming her.

"Would you like to come to Africa with me for a few weeks? Meet my friends. Visit my world."

"I would love that so much!"

"Then maybe, once we've had lots of fun and we trust each other implicitly and hone our communication skills, maybe we can talk about marriage?"

"That is the exact perfect thing to say, Mr. Black," Jane said, loving that he respected her cautious nature by taking things slow.

"I'm glad you agree, Ms. Grant."

"After Africa, maybe we can go visit your cousin Mitchell in Montana. I'd love to meet him and his new wife."

"I think that's a splendid idea." Then he wrapped his arms around her and pulled her into the fountain with him, and they came up laughing and sputtering.

As she kissed her cowboy, Jane couldn't help thinking that life with this larger-than-life man would never ever be boring.

Did you love *Arizona Heat*? Then you should read *Tomaz*[1] by Lori Wilde!

[2]

No-nonsense account executive Bianca St. James is determined to do what it takes to win the "summer of no sex" bet she's made with her three best friends. She's smart and capable and she always plays to win, but what Bianca doesn't count on is her billionaire client being so fiendishly hot.Professional bull rider Tomaz Santos has been at loose ends since retiring from the rodeo circuit and returning home to Brazil to take over his family swimwear business. He's learned the hard way how precious family is and he's not taking anything for granted.

---

1. https://books2read.com/u/3LyoNX
2. https://books2read.com/u/3LyoNX

Bianca is the woman this wealthy cowboy has been longing to know better, but she's determined to keep him at arm's length. Until one hot summer night when Tomaz convinces her to let go of work and just play...with him...

Read more at https://loriwilde.com.

Also by Lori Wilde

Cowboy Confidential

Cowboy Cop

Cowboy Protector

Cowboy Bounty Hunter

Cowboy Bodyguard

Cowboy Outlaw

Cowboy Country

Arizona Heat

Cowboy Rendezvous

Tomaz

Jake

Cody

Heartthrob Hospital

The Thunderbolt
The Jinx
The Hotshot

Kringle, Texas
A Perfect Christmas Gift
A Perfect Christmas Wish
A Perfect Christmas Surprise
A Perfect Christmas Joy
A Perfect Christmas Reunion

One Scorching Summer
Mr. Temptation
Mr. Temptation
Mr. Intoxicating
Mr. Undeniable
Mr. Scandalous

Texas Rascals
Keegan
Matt
Kurt
Tucker
Kael
Brodie
Dan

Rex
Clay
Jonah

Watch for more at https://loriwilde.com.

Also by Pam Andrews Hanson

Cowboy Country
Arizona Heat

About the Author

Lori Wilde is the New York Times, USA Today and Publishers' Weekly bestselling author of 85 works of romantic fiction. She's a three time Romance Writers' of America RITA finalist and has four times been nominated for Romantic Times Readers' Choice Award. She has won numerous other awards as well. Her books have been translated into 26 languages, with more than four million copies of her books sold worldwide. Her breakout novel, The First Love Cookie Club, has been optioned for a TV movie.

Lori is a registered nurse with a BSN from Texas Christian University. She holds a certificate in forensics, and is also a certified yoga instructor.

A fifth generation Texan, Lori lives with her husband, Bill, in the Cutting Horse Capital of the World; where they run

Epiphany Orchards, a writing/creativity retreat for the care and enrichment of the artistic soul.

Read more at https://loriwilde.com.

Printed in the USA
CPSIA information can be obtained
at www.ICGtesting.com
LVHW092132240224
772742LV00006B/81

9 798215 356869